BLOOD RIVER

Nightmare Vacations #1

Alexander Lane

Blood River by Alexander Lane.

Published by Hi3NichiNari.

www.alexanderlane.co.uk

Copyright © 2022 Alexander Lane.

This is a work of fiction. Names characters, places and incidents either are the products of the author's imagination or are used fictitiously. Any resemblance to actual persons, living or dead, businesses, companies, events or locales is entirely coincidental.

All rights reserved. No portion of this book may be reproduced in any form without permission from the publisher, except as permitted by British copyright law. For permissions contact rights@alexanderlane.co.uk.

Cover by Alexander Lane and Sharon Bruton.

ISBN: 978-1-7395830-1-9

To the dedicated people at the Orangutan Foundation UK who work tirelessly to protect the last orangutans living in the wild and gave me the opportunity to see their work first hand.

And to Sharon, who insists that I write.

HELP!

Sunday, August 19, 2018

Email: Imogen Nicholson to Alan Caudwell

To: alan@caudwell.org.uk
From: founder@saveorangutans.org.uk
Subject: help!
Date: 19 August 2018 11:27

Please help. I don't know who else I can turn to.

All of the staff and volunteers on the OST Summer Programme are missing. A dozen people have disappeared into the Borneo rainforest from Pondok Bahaya, a place you can only reach by boat on one river. I am hoping for the best but dreading the worst.

My staff are like a second family to me — you know that — and I'm responsible for our volunteers. I am desperate to find out what happened.

My rangers found diaries, mobile phones, a camera and a laptop when they reached the camp. But no clothes, no personal belongings.

I don't know where to start, but you know the area and you know our work. I know it's asking a lot, but could you look at them while my staff liaise with the authorities? You know how to put a story together and maybe you can find out where they've all gone.

Jenny

Email: Alan Caudwell to Imogen Nicholson

To: founder@saveorangutans.org.uk
From: alan@caudwell.org.uk
Subject: Re: help!
Date: 19 August 2018 13.16

Hi Jenny,

Of course. I'm already in Jakarta. I'll be back at my hotel in about an hour. I'll Skype from there — there's a flight to Pangkalanbun[1] tomorrow morning.

Best, Alan

---

[1] Pangkalanbun is a small town in Central Kalimatan, Indonesian Borneo. It has a major regional airport and provides river access to the forested interior, where there are few roads.

Join the Orangutan Survival Trust summer volunteer programme!

```
Editor's note: This is an extract from the
Orangutan Survival Trust web page advertising the
2018 summer project, provided for reference.
```

- **Help to save a magnificent species from extinction!**
- **Enjoy the adventure of a lifetime!**
- **Live in the most beautiful place on Earth!**

What is the Orangutan Survival Trust?

The Orangutan Survival Trust is a British charity dedicated to saving the last few remaining wild orangutans in Indonesian Borneo. We protect the rainforest on which they depend for survival, and the many other endangered species which share this habitat. This unique environment is threatened by logging, the spread of palm oil plantations and polluting mines.

The OST operates three private reserves adjoining the National Parks in Kalimantan, the southern half of Borneo belonging to Indonesia. Plantations, logging and mining are forbidden in these parks. Our rangers and those of the National Parks work to stop illegal logging and mining operations, while our conservation staff conduct essential research into the rainforest ecosystem and its inhabitants.

What is the Orangutan Survival Trust Summer Programme?

The Orangutan Survival Trust Summer Programme runs every year for three to six weeks at locations in Kalimantan.

As a volunteer, you will join OST staff at a site in one of our reserves or a National Park within Kalimantan, where you will work together to complete a specific construction goal in support of the rangers or conservation staff.

Previous Summer Programmes have refurbished guard posts for the rangers, constructed elevated walkways above the forest and swamp, and provided buildings for visitors to our research locations.

You may be invited to assist our staff in their field work and you will encounter indigenous wildlife in its natural habitat, including orangutans.

Our programme is ideal for wildlife photographers: you could get the picture of a lifetime!

What can I expect on the Orangutan Survival Trust Summer Programme?

Experience with hand tools is not required, but you should be sufficiently fit and healthy to complete a full day of work in the rainforest environment. As well as being very hot, the rainforest is extremely humid and you may find it uncomfortable for the first few days.

You should also be prepared for basic living conditions. This may involve sleeping in communal accommodation with your fellow volunteers, rudimentary toilet facilities and showering in cold water. We guarantee that you will become an expert in the art of the bucket shower!

We can also guarantee that you will have one of the most rewarding and memorable experiences of your life, making a significant contribution to our efforts to save the orangutans and their home.

Please apply by February 28, 2018.

ESCAPE

Saturday, July 21, 2018

Editor's note

At the request of the Orangutan Survival Trust's founder, Imogen Nicholson, I have compiled the surviving records of the Summer 2018 volunteer programme into an account which we believe explains the events which occurred at Pondok Bahaya. This account is intended for the confidential use of the trustees and other authorities investigating those events.

   Alan Caudwell, editor

Diary: Tara Fowler, evening

Tara, a businesswoman from Yorkshire, is taking part in her second Orangutan Survival Trust summer programme. This year she is the volunteer coordinator, responsible for liaising between the volunteers and OST staff, ensuring the volunteers are happy and healthy, and helping to manage the project.

It looks like she has bought a new journal for this trip, one which enables her to set out her plans and budget day-by-day — both personally and for the group — as well as recording her thoughts. Tara's handwriting is a neat and measured joined-up longhand that suggests she always thinks about the words she is writing and doesn't allow herself to be hurried by the need to write.

Two more nights and I'll be back in the rainforest! I feel like a little girl going on holiday, but it's just so so so good to be back in Borneo. Rendy's carefree face almost made me forget about all my crap at home when I got off the plane in PKB[2] today. He's so welcoming and excited about the programme and the new group of volunteers. After a few minutes it was all I wanted to think about too.

We had a busy day, meeting Pak Rafi — he's the Trust's general manager here and Rendy's boss — then shopping for fresh fruit and vegetables for the camp. Rendy bought me some Skittles — no melted Curly Wurly disasters this year!

All the while we were catching up on the gossip about his family and the camp staff. Dinner with Rendy and Pak Rafi tonight and an early start tomorrow to meet the volunteers at the airport. I should be exhausted from travelling but I'm so excited and happy to be here at last.

Diary: Rendy Dhanu Saradina, evening

This diary has been translated from Indonesian Bahasa.

Rendy is the project manager at Pondok Bahaya research station, which everyone usually calls 'the camp'. This personal diary was kept in a plain, lined, hardback notebook, and from the start date

---

[2] PKB — Pangkalanbun.

```
in June it looks like this was the second volume he
had used this year. The inside cover included
emergency contact details for the families of his
team members, as well as for his own family.
```

I do not often look forward to leaving the rainforest and coming to Pangkalanbun. It is a dirty town, either dusty in the dry season like this or muddy in the wet season. I love both seasons in the forest and I dislike them both here.

All the same, I was happy to be reunited with Tara today. I was impressed by her energy and organisation and positive attitude when she was a volunteer last year, so I am very pleased to have her coordinating the volunteers this year. She does not look any older or less beautiful, but there is something that has made her very unhappy. She has not talked about her partner at all and she was looking forward to buying a house with him last year. I think that in England this is almost as important as getting married here. Her personal life is none of my business, but I enjoy working with her and I hope that she finds her happiness again while she is in the forest. I know it is where I am the most happy.

I was very proud to tell her of my excellent new research assistant at Pondok Bahaya, young Dewi, and about Rangga, the new carpenter for this year's project.

We will have a lot to do in the next four weeks but I am confident that it can be done. I have wanted to rebuild the meeting hall since I arrived at Pondok Bahaya, so that we can bring in more people from all over Indonesia to learn about the wonderful plants and animals that are so close to them. I am sure that once they understand the rainforest, they will want to save it as much as I do.

Diary: Dewi Rifqi, evening

This diary has been translated from Indonesian Bahasa.

Dewi is a postgraduate researcher who has been at Pondok Bahaya for four months. Her diary, a blank-paged hardback notebook, includes many detailed sketches of local plants and animals. Leaves and flowers are pressed between many of its pages, accompanied by notes of when and where she found them.

Dewi has illustrated the inside cover with a pencil sketch of the camp, seen as you approach uphill from the dock on the Sungai Darah river. The wooden meeting hall is the size of small single-storey house, with a pitched metal roof. A veranda about four feet off the ground looks toward the river, with wide wooden steps at the centre. There's a single door in line with the steps, and a row of windows at chest-height surround the building. The steadily-climbing hillside meets the back of the meeting hall.

The forest has been cleared for about 10 feet around the right of the hall, making a path for people to go uphill towards the buildings behind. Only one of these is visible in Dewi's sketch — the long guest accommodation block. Like the meeting hall, it's raised from the ground with a veranda along the front, but this wooden building has a thatched roof and about 15 feet of cleared ground in front.

To the left of the hall, the forest comes within a few feet of the building, tall thin trees obscuring everything except the top of a water tower.

Bimo and Revo unloaded the lumber and cement and roofing this afternoon. I hope there will be enough to rebuild the meeting hall.

It is hard to believe that the hall is only 10 years old. It is as if the rainforest wants to reclaim anything we build. If you left this place for a few years even the concrete buildings would be covered in vines. I nearly put my foot through a hole in that ugly yellow plastic flooring today. We will have to put up a sign to warn the volunteers when they arrive.

I wonder what they will be like? Rendy says it is the first trip to Kalimantan for everyone apart from the coordinator, a woman called Tara. She sounds so bold and independent, coming halfway around the world on her own to help the orangutans. I know the Founder of the Orangutan Survival Trust did the same thing when she was my age, but I cannot imagine how she won the respect of so many men to achieve her goals. Britain must be a wonderful place for women.

Rendy is a wonderful boss, but I must also work with men like Bimo who only grunts at me when he needs something. I know he thinks I should be pumping out babies like the women he grew up with, but this is 2018. I want to have a career and make something of myself before I find a husband.

At least Revo can put a smile on anyone's face at the worst of times — even Bimo. And there are times when I am glad that Bimo is here, like this morning when a boat from the mining camp went past the dock. Revo said hello as he does to everyone, but Bimo just stared them down, and when Bimo stares you down it is very scary. If he was a dog you would hear him growling. The miners did not reply, but there was a young woman with them. She was crying and when she looked at us, one of the men shouted at her to look away. There is only one reason they would take a woman to the mining camp and it is not only to wash and cook. Everyone knows. Those men are animals. Sometimes I have nightmares that they will come here and take me away. We are very far away from anyone who can help us.

Revo and Rendy once took me just far enough up the river to see the mining camp. It is a wasteland. They chop down all the trees and poison everything else with chemicals to get their gold. Some of them are not even Indonesian. Sometimes I wish the mine would collapse on top of them. I know that is a horrible fate to wish on anyone, but those miners do not care about anyone. Rendy said the manager who was here before him tried to talk to them, but they threatened him. With guns! No one needs guns here unless they are going to hurt the wildlife. They are monsters.

The government should do something to close the mine but Rendy said it is owned by rich men who tell the politicians what to do. Why can they not stay away and leave the rainforest for the wildlife?

Email: Alan Caudwell to Imogen Nicholson

To: founder@savoorangutans.org.uk
From: alan@caudwell.org.uk
Subject: Pondok Bahaya diaries - July 21
Date: 23 August 2018 22:32

Jenny,

I promised to make a quick start — here's the first day of the diaries.

Your office in PKB was still under siege when I stopped to pick them up. Local media and stringers for the Western media are camped outside, but Pak Rafi is keeping them at bay. He's more concerned about reassuring the families of your missing staff, but I couldn't stay long — a European going into the OST office attracted far too much attention. I'm sure it's no easier for you in London and you must want to be here searching for your people, but I'm not sure that you would be able to achieve any more being here. I suppose that once the media get involved, it's all about the appearance of being hands-on.

I thought you might want to know a little about the state of the diaries when I received them. They'd been in a sealed plastic bag since they were found — Pak Rafi said he couldn't bear to read the diaries of his friends.

I've taken photos of the diaries to work from and handled them with gloves. I've sent the photos to a couple of colleagues to translate the Indonesian diaries and transcribe the rest — people I trust to keep things confidential. They're sending me daily updates so that I can keep them flowing to you.

The phones have gone to a guy who's fixed broken tech for me here before, and he's confident he can unlock them. It will be a lot to go through, but I'll send you more updates as soon as I can. I know it's not strictly legal, but they could be the key to finding out what happened.

As promised, Pak Rafi gave me a password for the laptop used by Rendy and Dewi, and I've been going through it while I waited for the transcriptions to start coming in. It's mostly camp admin but there are some pictures and videos from camera traps they placed in the rainforest. It looks like Dewi continued collecting them while the volunteers were there. Perhaps she saw something that will explain what happened?

Alan

Sunday, July 22, 2018

Whatsapp: Alison Pierce & Manny James

```
Alison Pierce's mobile phone included conversations
with her partner, Emmanuel James.
   I have included here the final conversation
between Alison (calling herself "Loose Ali") and
Emmanuel ("Manlymanny"). I believe it provides a
useful insight into her state of mind at the start
of her trip to Borneo.
```

Loose Ali: Hey Big Boy got 2 Borneo 2day. Last chance 2 leave me wanting more before I get 2 the jungle. So stinky and hot here. Im so sweaty and wet not in a good way 😜 🫣

Manlymanny: Tease!!!! Thought i gave u plenty. Cant believe Im loosing u to a bunch of monkeys

Loose Ali: Lol u gave me some good memories. Anyway told you there not monkeys there apes. Just like u but better lookin 😜

Manlymanny: Not all ur there 4. I no u never miss out on a holiday shag

Loose Ali: Got 2 be a good grl 4 a month or theyll send me home

Manlymanny: U wont last a week if theres someone u want. U cant say no. Lucky if I can tap u twice a week as it is.

Loose Ali: Can't help myself u know what I'm like. So many flavas 4 1 girl to try. Don't give most cocks 2 rides so u no ur special.

Manlymanny: 2 right. I no u say rootings the only thing dat keeps ur brain quiet so u do what u have 2 do.

Loose Ali: Only 2 other blokes here. Ones an old gay but I would ride the young one. Local blokes off limits. Might have to lezz up. Save something 4 me. I no u cant keep it in ur pants 4 a month lol.

Manlymanny: Cant wait to read ur lesbo adventures. Ill have enough for u when u get back. Ull need another holiday when i finish with u.

Loose Ali: Haha you wish. Now send me a pic of that beast so I know what I'm missing.

Manlymanny: Ur fones got more cocks than a chicken farm. Want 2 see u sweaty.

Loose Ali: No chance. Shared room with a kid. Ud like her. Big eyes big smile big ass. Nowhere 4 pics though. Use ur brain haha

Manlymanny: Lol u don't need that. Want a pic of u both and ill tell u what ill do 2 her.

Loose Ali: OK will send later. Make it nasty.

Manlymanny: OK haha nothings 2 nasty 4 u. Dont feel bad if u have 2 help urself x

Diary: Dewi Rifqi, evening

Pondok Bahaya is ready for our guests! It will be very exciting to have all of these new people here later today and to show them this beautiful place.

Today I finished helping Ibu Intan set up her new kitchen. She is a little unhappy at moving out of the old building into a tent, but she knows she will be getting a new kitchen in a few weeks when the volunteers have finished. She is just like my lovely old auntie, and it is good to have another woman to talk to.

Rangga, the new carpenter, arrived this morning. He made friends with the men when he was inspecting the lumber. I said hello but I have not had time to speak to him for long. I will have to ask Ibu Intan about him. He has a nice smile and looks like a hard worker.

That female orang and her baby went past the camp again this morning. She always stops to have a look at us but she gets very angry if anyone goes near to her, even though they are far up in the trees. The baby does not seem to even notice us. He just reaches out for any fruit he can see. I have heard some male calls again today but I do not think she was moving towards them, not with a baby. The volunteers will be very excited if they can see an orang in the wild. What am I saying? I am always excited when I see them!

I had another good surprise last night when my old friends Liani and Putri came up the river with a family of tourists. I think they were from Germany. We had time to catch up on our gossip. It seems like so long since we were at school together and they are both making a lot of money from showing tourists around the forest. Visitors trust the female guides more than the men, especially the families who have come all of the way here from Europe or America. I know some of the men resent us, like Bimo does. I wonder what will happen to Putri when she marries that teacher? She must be earning more than him. Liani needs to be careful with that boat-captain. Everyone knows he has women up and down the river! He does not mind women working if they bring him customers, at least. They teased me a little about Rendy but I tell them he is just my boss, as always.

This afternoon I set up some new camera traps. I love being in the forest on my own. I have seen Bimo raise his eyebrows, even Revo and Rendy, but I do not care. I know there are dangerous creatures out there, but I know how to move carefully and most animals will avoid humans. I breathe in deeply and I can feel the life all around me. I can almost see the trees growing and the flowers waiting to bloom. The clever little mouse deer watching me through the undergrowth. I imagine a clouded leopard resting in the trees, one eye open for prey. The only thing I do not want to meet is a big monitor lizard. Everyone has one animal that makes their spine go cold.

There were strange footprints in the floor near one of my cameras. Monkey footprints, perhaps, but monkeys do not travel alone and these were larger than I would expect. It could be a solo male orangutan — they come down to look at the camera traps sometimes. I would love to see one of those, but they can be dangerous. How exciting!

I am anxious to go through the memory cards and see what I find this time. It will be a reward for the volunteers to show them photos and videos from the camera traps when we have built the new hall. We even have video of a clouded leopard which no-one outside the camp has yet seen.

I feel like reading Reflections of Eden again tonight. Rendy says he will have to buy me a new copy when this one falls apart. I wish I had been here with Biruté Galdikas when it was all unspoiled. It must have been so exciting for her.

Diary: Tara Fowler, night

One more night and I'll be back in the rainforest! Tomorrow morning we'll be getting out of dusty Pangkalanbun and onto a boat for a lazy trip up the river to Pondok Bahaya. What is it Rendy calls it? A klotok! If it's anything like last year I'll be calling all the boats klotoks in a couple of days.

Organising the volunteers isn't quite the same as running my own business at home. I didn't hire these people for a start: they're volunteers and all I knew about them until this morning was from their application forms and a few chats on Facebook. I know

Rendy's really the one in charge but I'm still responsible for them — they'll talk to me first until they get to know him, at least if they're anything like me when I got here.

They're a mixed bag — a young student, a teacher who's about my age, a retired teacher, a middle-aged American woman and an Australian guy in his 20s. Apart from him I think most of them are getting used to the crazy heat. They had more questions about the toilets and the living accommodation at the camp than anything else. I remember feeling like that when I got here last year.

It'll be a bonus to have no more wifi when we leave the hotel. Bloody Jason won't stop setting up those bogus email accounts to call me names and threaten me. I feel better every minute I get further away from that bastard. I've never been one to feel scared and I hate the way he made me feel after that time with the kitchen knife. I still feel like a fool for being taken in by that charming, easygoing guy I worked with. It just goes to show that you should never date a colleague. He's out of my life and it will be a new start when I get back.

Instagram: Cristian Jarvis

Cristian Jarvis is the only volunteer who did not keep a diary during the programme, but he did take a lot of photos and videos for his two Instagram accounts and for photography competitions, both using his phone and an expensive Nikon digital camera.

The @pecstourist Instagram account has become infamous for its selfies of Cristian posing to show off his physique, often alongside women who were his sexual partners or with whom he expected to become intimate. Many of the images on @pecstourist push the limits of Instagram's taste and decency guidelines, and many have been removed since the account rose to its current notoriety.

Cristian's other Instagram account is @junglelover. It is focused on wildlife photography, and records him having won some minor awards for his work.

Cristian's phone also contained hundreds of unpublished images and videos, including numerous sexually explicit records of relationships prior to these events.

While at Pondok Bahaya, Cristian has prepared several photos for @pecstourist, complete with captions and hashtags, although this was the only one uploaded from Borneo before the group entered the rainforest. It's a selfie with Maya Pollard from the river port of Pangkalanbun, taken with a selfie stick in front of a wide river in bright sunshine.

Cristian, who's 25 years old, is a tall man with a physique that has spent a lot of time in the gym. He has dark hair, streaked with blonde, and a short beard. Maya is a younger woman of average build, weight and height, her hair dyed a platinum blonde and tied back, but she's wearing no make-up. They are standing, wearing sunglasses. She's blowing a kiss to the camera, her arms outstretched, wearing long trousers and a loose but modest top. He is laughing, one arm around her shoulders, wearing shorts and a sleeveless shirt with the logo of an Australian football team.

@pecstourist snagged a hottie for the jungle 🌿 🐒 #30days #summer2018 #hot #henchwoman #itsgonnahappen #junglehot #blonde #girl #sexy #student #20 #lookingcute #jungle_fashion #tropical_fashion #follow #followme #instafollow #like4likes

Email: Imogen Nicholson to Alan Caudwell

To: alan@caudwell.org.uk
From: founder@saveorangutans.org.uk
Subject: Re: Pondok Bahaya diaries - July 22
Date: 24 August 2018 18:29

Alan,

A second batch already! Thank you — again — for working so fast on these diaries. It is reassuring to have someone in PKB who can do this while poor Pak Rafi attracts all of the publicity.

The media here has wasted no time digging into the social media accounts of our volunteers. It must be a living nightmare for their families. Of course we are being criticised for letting someone like Cristian join the programme. All I can say is that we believed that his desire to save the orangutans was genuine. We don't have the time or staff to trawl through the social media accounts of everyone who applies. I wish we did.

Apologies for the rant. It's not fair to talk to anyone outside the organisation about what's happened, and everyone here needs me to keep my head. I'm trying to find a professional who will help us to deal with the public relations nightmare, but it feels as though we are so toxic that no-one will help us pro bono and we cannot afford to hire anyone.

Jenny

Monday, July 23, 2018

Email: Maya Pollard to Madeline Jones

This was the last email sent by Maya Pollard before leaving the hotel in Pangkalanbun. It was delivered to Madeline Jones, a close friend and fellow student at the University of Canterbury, England, and was recovered from Maya's mobile phone.

As with Alison Pierce's WhatsApp, I believe it provides an insight into this young woman's state of mind as she looked forward to the adventure of a lifetime.

From: maya1997@gmail.com
To: mjones1998@kent.ac.uk
Subject: OMG orangutans tomorrow!!!
Date: 24 July 2018 07:11

Hey Maddie! Woke up early n thought Id say bye before we get on the boat… Cant believe Im here in Borneo…this is nothing like going to greece in May. I know I love orangutans but can't believe I might see them tomorrow.

Haven't seen much jungle yet but its hot and I don't mean holiday hot where you can laze around. Glad we're only in this town for one night...not much to do and the shops are so strange even going to the supermarket is like something new. Got some more snacks and biscuits but Im not sure what they all are guess Ill find out haha

Heathrow was so big on my own and they give you free drink ont he plane...well, you cant drink here so I thought I might as well have as much as I could before I go dry for a month haha. Slept like a log after my second little vino lol. I met most of the others at the airport this morning before we came here...its nothing like uni or home babe...there are two old people and this girl whos done like loads of travelling...the one in that selfie I sent you...shes my roomie here before we go up the river but last night she told me shes really nervous about going so long without been able to to whatsapp her fam and boyf...she msgs him a lot...Ill miss u and my fam but not that much lol xx

The olds are ok but the things they find funny Im like wtf is that? The girl in charge Tara is OK shes done this before and she knows whats going on but I think me n Cristian pissed her off when we were larfin at things in the bus last night. Hes a few years older than me n hes been like everywhere but hes funny AF so at least Ill have someone to kid with. Its obv he wants me n hes hench n all so I might save him until the end of the trip in case it gets boring. Fran thinks were still on when I get back to uni but honestly like I told u I dont know if I can be bothered with his nonsense next year if it means I cant have fun on my hols.

Roomie must be missing her boyf...think she was sextng last night when she thought I was aslepp yeuch! shes got 50 Shades of grey in her bag wtaf lol

Right gotta go n get brekfast or whatever it is they have here. I hope theres coco pops. Bad enough no beer for a month

See you in a few weeks babe xx

***

From: maya1997@gmail.com
To: mjones1998@kent.ac.uk
Subject: NO COCO POPS :'(
Date: 24 July 2018 07:52

NO COCO POPS some spicy shit and ckaes for breakfast wtf? At least they have coffee. Tara said were going to see orangutans get fed before we get to the camp tonight!!! How cool is that? Cool AF I say xx wish I could send you pics but NO MORE INTERNET noooooo loool xx

Letter: Alison Pierce to Manny James

Alison Pierce's diary is a leather-bound deep pink notebook which has been custom-bound with "Ali's Exotic Adventures: Borneo" on the front cover. The first page contains a message in neat, male handwriting: "For all your adventures, dreams and fantasies. I hope they all come true. Keeping your bed warm, Manny xoxo".

The diary is themed around exploring the natural world, with pages interrupted by quotes and drawings from famous naturalists and maps of exotic locations. Alison adds a new date to the start of every page, and has drawn cute, friendly animals, plants and trees around the quotes, embellishing them sparingly.

Alison's joined-up handwriting is busy — full of loops and curls, but it reflects her emotional state almost line-by-line, flowing smoothly when she's happy, becoming more jagged (and difficult to read) when she's unhappy, and meandering into loops around names when she writes about sex. A chunk of the diary at the back has been torn out.

Rather than a typical diary of daily entries, Alison writes letters to her partner which mingle daily observations on her trip with explicit erotic adventures and fantasies to read on her return. It seems likely that she did this every time she went travelling alone. Where possible, I have excluded the intimate and pornographic details. These excisions are marked with […]

Hey sexy,

Thanks for the diary babe. More Exotic Adventures! We know it's my erotic adventures you want to hear about lol

You might get lucky — don't you always ;) There's a dirty hunk I've got my eye on. Have to steal him from that little student. She teased him all the way here. I'll show him what an older woman can do. Wouldn't mind teaching her a thing or two. Bet you'd love to read about that! […]

Saw a few other big men on the way here haha they were all orangutans at Camp Pail. It's the oldest sanctuary in Borneo. They feed the orangutans they've rescued and released back into the jungle where it's safe. SO BIG and beautiful and powerful. Oh! The smell of their fur. A young male came right down a tree next to where I was standing. Looked me straight in the eye. I breathed in to scream. Just got this thick, heavy smell. Talk about the smell of a real man!! He huffed at me before the wardens shooed him away. I almost huffed back!!!! Had so many tingles I couldn't move or stop grinning for ages. […]

Paul — this sweet old gay geezer on the trip — even asked if I was OK. Know you said I was crazy coming out here to the dirty jungle. It's so lovely too. Really really want to enjoy myself.

We're on a big old slow boat to Pondok Bahaya for tonight. Wish you were here. Now that would be an exotic adventure!!!! […]

Thinking loose thoughts, Ali

Diary: Paul Dickerson, night

```
Paul Dickerson's diary is an expensive green
Moleskine, neatly labelled with his contact
details. His elegant, flowing handwriting is a
pleasure to read. It was obviously bought well in
advance of the programme, and contains detailed
travel plans and budgets alongside several pages of
notes on plants and wildlife that Paul hoped to see
in Borneo.
```

Orangutans! Real live orangutans!

It is difficult to describe the beauty of the rainforest if you have never seen anything like it. There is something wonderfully romantic in the idea that we are somewhere that you can only reach by boat, or klotok as they call them here (I am not sure whether a klotok is a big boat or a small one). Our boat, thankfully, was a big one, with a covered top deck, open on the sides so that we could enjoy the view, with a downstairs deck for the crew and kitchen.

We set out early this morning from a small port called Kumai[3], on a vast river that must have been a couple of miles from bank to bank. It took us half an hour to cross it, but we soon turned off onto a much smaller river, and it got more and more narrow all the way up to Pondok Bahaya — that's our camp for the next month. Sometimes the trees brushed against both sides of the boat, and there was just enough room for it to turn around by the dock here. We are about as far up the river as a boat of this size can go, I would say.

```
³ Kumai is a river port, approximately 45 minutes' drive
east of Pangkalanbun.
It is the principal port of departure for tourists visiting
Camp Pail and the surrounding national park, as well as for
OST staff and visitors to the charity's reserve adjoining
the national park.
```

The colour of the river was a real shock: when we came off the main river it started to change colour from a muddy brown to a rich, dark red-brown. Rendy told me that's why they call it the Sungai Darah: it literally means 'Blood River', but it's because of the silt that washes down from the hills where it starts. He said it was easier for the OST to set up their forest reservation on the river because the indigenous people stay away from the water and the oil palm trees don't grow as well here, so the land was cheap.

The rainforest is thick to the water's edge and the trees are enormous. There were places where they leaned across the river and met in the middle. Most of them aren't that broad, but they reach up into the sky — at least 100 feet according to Rendy. Every so often you will glimpse monkeys sitting in the trees, families of up to a dozen, and if you're lucky there will be one or two orangutans for an hour or two of travelling along the river. Thankfully our journey here lasted more than six hours so we were treated very generously with sights of both. We also saw houses on stilts along the river bank, though not many, and a few people fishing on the river.

Our big boat went back down the river after we got off and they unloaded a lot of supplies. There are just a couple of long wooden canoes with outboard motors that I suppose the staff use to get about. I hope we get to ride in them, although I shall keep my hands out of the water. Who knows what lurks beneath? Crocodiles? Or is it alligators they have here?

It is quite thrilling to know that we are almost cut off for the next few weeks. I shall miss Jerry of course, but I am already pleased that my phone has not beeped or rung since we left the hotel. The joy of isolation!

We stopped on the way to Pondok Bahaya at the famous Camp Pail. It's where they first started to study orangutans in Kalimantan, and we saw them feed orangutans who have been released into the wild. The big surprise for me was that the place was so full up with tourists. I had no idea that so many people come here on holiday. Most of them are on day trips from the town we stayed in last night, and the boats filled up the river from one side to the other when we arrived.

The man in charge of us is a lovely chap called Rendy. I don't think he liked the tourists at Camp Pail very much, but I suppose it helps people to see the orangutans as wild animals and pays for the conservation work they do here.

There was a platform just about twenty feet away from us. As soon as the staff put a huge pile of bananas on it, the trees started rustling with orangs moving in. You could see the trees bending as they swung from one to the next, and it was obvious that they had been waiting nearby. They are such beautiful creatures, so graceful when they swing from tree to tree and so strong, but they're ridiculously funny when they have a mouth stuffed full of bananas. Their arms and legs just seem to go on forever when they reach out for a branch but on the ground they just seem the right length for their bodies. All the tourists stopped talking and we just stared in awe at the orangs.

The mothers came to feed with their babies first. They're so caring and watchful over them and the young ones only go as far as they feel safe. Sometimes it's not very far at all! The males came in later, but none of the big males with the flanges on their faces. I know they're very rare but I'm here for a month so maybe we'll get a special visit! Alison — one of the other volunteers here — had a bit of a close encounter with one of them and she was just struck dumb by it. I don't blame her!

The orangs didn't stay long — just filled their faces with bananas and went up a tree to eat them. It was almost raining banana skins, they eat them so fast. Then they came back down and put as many bananas in their mouths as they could again. I was simply not prepared for it. They are so wonderful and so funny as well. I didn't know whether to laugh or cry. So I did both.

The staff don't let the orangs come too close when they get curious about people, which they do, especially the mothers and babies. They have such intelligence in those deep eyes and their fur is so wonderful, such a deep orange and yet clean of twigs and leaves. I don't know how they do it! I know I have seen them countless times at London Zoo, but I honestly don't think I could go there again after this. Just seeing them come down from those great trees, then climb back up again and disappear into the forest, you get an idea of the vast amount of space they need to live in. It can't be right to keep groups of them close together in a cage. Even the good zoos can't give them the sort of space they have here in the wild.

Many people, too many for my liking, tried to take selfies but the orangs were too far away. That includes my young room-mate for the next few weeks, Cristian. I think he will be quite the handful!

He is like a dog in heat for all the women in the group, although I have a feeling he would screw anything with a pulse. I am not interested but we have all met men like that! He has focussed his attention on the youngest woman, Maya, but you can tell that he will take any opportunity and he is not embarrassed about it. I think that she is quite happy to flirt with him, and he is attractive in that surfer-dude fashion, although I am not sure she will take it as far as he would like. She may have some competition from Alison, who is also flirty, but I think he prefers the younger women. In my experience, younger women are more easily impressed by such antics.

Cristian and I must share a room and get along, so provided that he doesn't try to bring one of them in here I think we will be fine. I do not think he is that brazen, though. He did help me to put up my mosquito net so I should be generous to him until we have got to know each other. He is sitting in his bed now, listening to music on his headphones and preparing photographs for his Instagram account. Apparently, he has quite the following.

Diary: Rendy Dhanu Saradina, night

The volunteers have all arrived safely and are in the camp, ready to begin work on this year's summer project. Well, it is summer for them. For us, it is the hotter and more humid time before the rains arrive, although that could be sooner than usual this year. The monsoon happens earlier each year in this part of the world. Perhaps it is because there is so little rainforest left to absorb the heat and moisture. I know there is less and less every year, and it is so hard to keep the loggers out of our parks.

Dewi assures me that all of the supplies have arrived for the next few weeks. I am sure we will be needing more nails — Rangga has not seen how many the volunteers throw away before they learn how to drive a nail into the ironwood. It will not be a problem. They are easy to fetch and we usually need water, vegetables and treats for the volunteers once a week. The presence of a female orangutan is very promising for the volunteers. Even breaking out a packet of biscuits in week three does not put more smiles on their faces than seeing an orangutan.

Tara has not spoken about her situation at home, but I could see her become more relaxed as the boat set off from Kumai. Tara, Paul and Harriet did not watch the signal bars disappear on their mobile phones as the boat set off. Cristian, Maya and Alison were all trying to send final messages.

Harriet is the first American I have had on the volunteer programme, so I do not know if they all have voices which reach every corner of the jungle. I am sure that before the programme is complete we will come to know her opinion on every topic and every bug in the forest. But it has been a long time since I saw someone cry with joy when they first saw an orangutan mother and baby. My mother would say that she has a wealthy figure, and I hope that she will not find the work here too difficult. I have no doubt she will leave here a little poorer.

Paul was also close to tears at Camp Pail. He is very observant of people and speaks in a gentle, clear voice. I think he may be a homosexual, which I have always been told is bad but it is accepted in the UK. It is probably best that Bimo does not find out. I do not want him to become sullen with any of the volunteers or to have any accidents with hammers.

Alison smiled like a child when she saw the orangutans at Camp Pail, so it was a shame that she did not have a good start this evening. She stepped in a hole in the floor, despite the sign that Dewi had placed to warn us of the danger. Thankfully Cristian was quick to pull her back. Tomorrow will not be too soon to begin demolishing that building.

We may have to be wary of Cristian and Maya creating a scandal. They are very much like the young people we had last year. I saw men like Cristian when I grew up in Jakarta. Young women are not able to resist their charm and promises, and I do not think that she wishes to resist very much. It may offend Bimo and Ibu Intan, and there was a similar issue last year with some volunteers of a similar age.

I understand that young people in Europe are not used to hiding their passion, so if it persists I will ask Tara to remind them that they must respect our society. A gentle warning was enough to prevent any scandal last year and they discovered that the rainforest is large enough for anyone to find privacy from other people, if not from ants and spiders. I am confident that The Founder always sends us good people and I wish for everyone to enjoy the programme.

Instagram: Cristian Jarvis

Cristian's second scheduled image displayed the female volunteers in a group on the sundeck of a klotok. He's contrived the photo to show Maya and Alison at the front, with Tara and Harriet behind them. Maya is relaxed, pulling a playful duckface. Alison wears a look of flirty disdain. Tara is ignoring the camera while Harriet's scowl is unintentionally comical.

@pecstourist Borneo henches are fighting for the pecs. I win every way 😜 #hotinthejjungle #hotties #henchwomen #itsgonnahappen #junglehot #blonde #girl #sexy #student #just20 #brunette #playingitcool #experienced #hungry #bitchfight #girlfight #theywantsome #Iwin #player #playa #gottacatchthemall #workingit

It would be unfair to say that Cristian's eyes were entirely focussed on Maya and Alison on the journey to Pondok Bahaya.

His phone and camera held thousands of photos of orangutans, birds and wildlife spotted along the banks of the river, and Maya seems to have been entirely forgotten when they visited the orangutans at Camp Pail. Alison only appears by accident as a young male orangutan descends from the trees to the ground in front of her. Her face is a portrait of enraptured — almost transcendent — delight.

Email: Alan Caudwell to Imogen Nicholson

To: founder@saveorangutans.org.uk
From: alan@caudwell.org.uk
Subject: Pondok Bahaya diaries - July 23
Date: 25 August 2018 09:17

Jenny,

Don't feel bad about the rant. You're in a terrible position, and to be honest I'm quite enjoying the skullduggery of being your secret agent in Borneo.

I have known you long enough to be sure that you wouldn't allow anyone unsuitable onto one of these projects, but I've been reading Cristian's Instagram feed and he seems like a complete prick! I'm sure his countrymen would have a very special term for him. The media will have a field day when those women start talking, and you can be sure that some of them will! At least everyone else seems fairly normal, although I wouldn't be surprised if Alison has a few skeletons in her closet.

Don't hesitate to send me another rant if you need to let off steam. Stay strong!

Alan x

Tuesday, July 24, 2018

Diary: Paul Dickerson, night

The first day in camp has been exhausting, but I think that I will survive.

Our breakfast was porridge, of all things, with sugar and powdered chocolate to flavour. And tea, thank goodness. The porridge was surprisingly good, in a nostalgic way. I think we will all be glad of a filling start to the day from now on.

Our introduction to jungle labour was a brief talk about health and safety: wear gloves; wear goggles if you can stand them in the heat (I can't); lots of sunscreen and water; stop if you feel tired. Wear heavy shoes even if the Indonesians don't bother.

Cristian was put to good work showing off as he joined Tara and some of the Indonesians at pulling the wall planks off the main hall. We're eating outside from now on!

The rest of us were sawing and chiselling posts that I vaguely understand are for joists. There was frequent intervention from Rangga, our foreman, and Revo, who I think is an all-round handyman and research assistant. All of it good-natured, I'm pleased to say. Neither of them speak English, but Rangga is adept at communicating with his hands and Revo chuckles patiently as we follow his examples. I noticed them tidying up our crude work while we ate lunch! They'd probably finish this much faster without us, but that's not the point, is it?

The meals have been simple stir-fried vegetables with copious rice and noodles. Our cook is called Ibu Intan, a middle-aged lady with not a word of English and only a few more teeth, but a remarkable gift for flavour. I think she's holding back on the spice for now, though.

Conversations so far have been very much about what we do and where we're from, with nothing remarkable to report. Everyone was tired from the 6am start and the manual labour, so after-dinner chat did not last long. Even the flirtation between Cristian and Maya was subdued this evening, although I think he has enough energy for two.

The other volunteers are all women. I think I will get along very well with Harriet. She has a joyful sense of humour and was almost beside herself when the orangutans were being fed. I cannot wait until they turn up in the camp — both to see them and to see her! Her reaction to the bugs in the room she shares with Tara was expressive, to say the least, but I think she is just in the habit of letting her thoughts find their voice. I am sure she was only voicing what most of us were thinking! She's not pleased about the loss of our communal dining and seating area, either, now that the meeting hall is being rebuilt. Well, I know I didn't come here expecting home comforts.

Tara is our group coordinator. She is very organised and pleasant, has a calm head and clearly has a great rapport with our leader, Rendy. You could not meet a more charming young man. He obviously cares a great deal for all of the wildlife and the rainforest, but he made sure to talk to everyone on the journey here, even though we were all very distracted looking for orangs, monkeys and birds in the trees along the river. He was so quick to see them, but I suppose that is what happens when you live here for months or years.

Young Maya is very pretty, even without the dramatic makeup she wore when we flew in yesterday. She was very chatty and excited on the boat here and seems to be quite bright, although when she is with Cristian they fall into silliness and flirting.

Alison, I spotted as a fellow educator from the moment we met. She is a science teacher so I am sure this will be very valuable to her. It turns out that we both have the book that Imogen Nicholson wrote about founding the OFI. Rendy has a copy in his office here — the staff all worship that woman — they call her "The Founder". I am sure Alison and I will have much to talk about and she was almost as excited as myself when the orangutans arrived. There's a tension in her, too, as though she's struggling with something inside while she puts on a brave face. Most likely it's the heat and mosquitoes.

I have the impression that she would have welcomed some of the attention that Cristian lavishes on young Maya. I don't believe she's above a little subterfuge to get it, either. There was a moment this evening when Alison stepped into a hole in the floor of the hall and Cristian caught her before she fell through. She gave quite a scream, but I wonder that the rest of us saw the warning sign and she did not. The incident occurred precisely when Cristian was on hand to save her. It would not be the first time I have seen a woman engineer a crisis to flatter her saviour. I would say that she felt it had the desired effect.

I want to record a little bit about the place where we are staying before I go to sleep as well.

Our camp is not large, although Tara tells us that it is large compared to the camp on her last visit. The jetty continues about one hundred yards inland, sloping uphill into the forest before it opens up into the main camp. There is a short climb up into the camp, but it is a treacherous place where you have to step on tree roots that have been exposed by people walking in and out. The Indonesians hopped up the hill in flip-flops, but we will have to be careful until we get used to it. Jerry would probably call the council to complain!

The jungle presses in on the camp from every direction and keeps us in the shade for most of the day. I do not imagine that I will see a sunrise or sunset until we leave. The air is very humid, but it smells wonderfully earthy and organic. I am not sure those are the best words, but I have never smelled anything so utterly natural.

The main building is a large wooden hall. This is what we shall be rebuilding for the next few weeks. Behind this, there is an awning set up for the kitchen, a small concrete accommodation block for the staff, an office and the long wooden accommodation block for the volunteers like me. The wooden buildings are painted in blue and green — they could do with a fresh coat of paint but the faded glamour makes me like this place even more. There are four rooms in our block, each with a bunk bed, so we will have a little privacy, and a covered veranda runs along the front of the block. There is also a toilet block with two rooms where we can shower and wash our clothes. I have a feeling that we will be showering twice a day at the start and not at all by the end of our stay! Tara seems to consider it the height of luxury. Apparently last year's toilets were far more basic.

One thing that no-one prepared me for was the noise of the jungle at night. The nocturnal wildlife is far louder than the daytime creatures. I am glad that Jerry put those earplugs in my bags.

Letter: Alison Pierce to Manny James

Hey my hot Manny,

Want you here to help me sleep! Think I got about an hour last night!! Soooo bored!!! Jungle noise is no better than all those crazy thoughts running through my head non-stop. Was hoping they'd cancel out. Leave me in peace. Haven't got enough books to be up all night every night. Only so much time I can spend writing about what I'd like to do to Maya and that big Ozzie guy. Still thinking about that orangutan from yesterday babe. Maybe I should buy you an ape suit when I come home! […] Still can't entertain myself like I would at home — not with her sleeping in the top bunk. Tried last night and woke her up. Had to pretend I was having a bad dream!

Had to do something today to keep up with Maya flirting with Cristian. He flirts with me too but men love it when a pretty little thing like her gets interested. Cristian spent the day flexing his muscles. Maya ogling and giggling like a teenager. Just because she's a bit younger. I'm only 32 FFS!

First took a pic of him pulling old planks off the walls of the hall we're restoring. Showed it to him this afternoon. Maya was having her post-work shower (shower sex here would be filth babe) […]. Says he'll put it on his Insta! I'll wait til he gets bored with the little girl (not SO little anyway haha).

Tonight got him to grab me when I almost fell in a hole in the floor. Saw a sign warning about it. Thought it would be fun to step in just as Cristian was walking past. The young woman scientist who works here — Duey, or Dooey or something weird — she tried to warn me. Pretended not to hear her. My foot went straight through the floor. The hole was fucking huge!!! Screamed a bit more than I planned to but it worked haha Big arms wrapped round me and picked me up. Said thanks with a lil' wink. He knows what I mean.

Maya still talking about Cris though. She didn't catch our vibe. Cris this, Cris that. He's next door FFS. Keep telling the kid he can probably hear everything she's saying. She won't shut up. Takes my mind off the beasts buzzing and screeching and croaking outside. TBH he probably CAN'T hear us over that.

Not sure the Indonesians sleep much. Men seem to stay up talking and smoking until we go to bed. Old woman who cooks for us was up at about 4AM when I went to the toilet! Not complaining. Soooo spooky outside in the dark with just my head torch.

50 shades was the wrong book to take my mind off you. Might have to go for a walk around the camp or I'll go mad lying in bed all night. No! It's too freaky out there at night!!

Mad n horny Ali xx

Instagram: Cristian Jarvis

```
Cristian made sure that his Instagram followers
enjoyed his good looks as well as his conquests,
and he wasted no time setting up a shot in Pondok
Bahaya.

  According to the caption, Alison took this photo
of him crowbarring an old board from the wall of
the main hall, topless and in shorts that are more
suited to the beach than the jungle. His impressive
physique and gleaming smile are shown off to great
effect, I suspect as much for the immediate
audience as for his followers.
```

@pecstourist Jungle hottie Ali couldn't wait to snap me when she got a load of the #pecs and #quads. This jungle monkey practically threw herself at me last night, but which one will scream the loudest? Only one way to find out 🐒 🍆 #hotinthejungle #hotties #henchwomen #timetoplay #fourweeksoffun #experienced #brunette #athletic #teacher #badteacher #naughtygirl

Email: Imogen Nicholson to Alan Caudwell

To: alan@caudwell.org.uk
From: founder@saveorangutans.org.uk
Subject: Re: Pondok Bahaya diaries - July 24
Date: 26 August 2018 12:11

Alan,

Your prediction about Cristian didn't need long to be proved correct — that poor girl in Australia that he left with a child after university. I can't believe his father just paid her off like that. He doesn't seem like a very pleasant character, either. I'm beginning to wonder how much of anything Cristian told us was true.

He had told us about the @junglelover Instagram account and I thought it showed some excellent nature photography. Perhaps I should have been suspicious that some of those photos were taken at the kind of nature parks where they drug and hobble the animals to make it easy for tourists to pose with them, and now I have seen some of the same women posing on his other account with a lot less to cover them. He seemed to have a professional photographer's talent for putting people at ease and delivering great photos. At ease is one way to put it! Were these women a fringe benefit of his nature photography, or was the photography an easy way to meet them in a relaxed setting?

We're lucky Cristian only posted one picture from Borneo on that other account. I do hope that young Maya didn't "hook up" with him or whatever they call it these days. She seems like such a nice girl, but I suppose we were all young once, eh? ;) Even if she did, the things people say about her in their comments — about all of those women — it makes me so angry. Why do the women get all the abuse?

On a positive note, I have found someone who might help us to deal with the media and give me more time to communicate with the volunteers' families. My phone is ringing night and day, then there are emails and texts and all of the social media to deal with. Much of it is supportive but there are already people accusing us of putting our volunteers in danger or selling access to the orangutans under the guise of conservation. Where do they get these horrible ideas? I've told the team here to stop responding.

We have so little information that I just don't know what to say to the families, let alone to the press. If this PR person works out, I'll fly over so I can talk to the police about giving us more information. They've had days at the site now — there must be something they can tell us, but Pak Rafi says even his old friends in the park rangers have been told not to talk to us.

Our book! Do you remember the fun we had writing it? I wish they wouldn't call me The Founder. I tried to stop it but Pak Rafi frowns if anyone calls me Ms Nicholson. I think he'd explode if they said my first name.

It will be good to catch up when I get there.

Jenny x

Wednesday, July 25, 2018

Letter: Alison Pierce to Manny James

Mmmmmanny!

I know you like that one!

Another day watching Cris and Maya flirt. Another night awake on my own. What I wouldn't do for a few G&Ts and a quick fuck.

I know when to back off. Think I'd really like Maya but she's hogging the only free man. Sure she's just teasing Cristian for fun. Not fair on a girl with my needs. Pretty little cockblocker.

Chatting before bed about the trip here. Maya reminds me of when I first rolled up in Thailand when I was 21. She's never done anything like this. Only been to Greece and Spain with her friends. Started telling her about all of the places I've been. None of them were anything like this. She got that faraway travel bug look in her eyes. The one you love. Didn't even tell her the hot stuff I write about for you. […]

Mozzies here are crazy. You know I love travelling but hate mozzies. Never been anywhere with mozzie screens this bad. So many holes. Don't stop anything. Glad I've got a proper mozzie net at least. Bitten like 20 times at dinner tonight. Smothered in DEET[4] all the time. Gets in my food. Skin feels like I'm cooking for the first half hour. And it's so hot at night! Wish I could sleep naked but I'd get bitten to fuck in five minutes.

Don't know how Tara can sleep outside in a hammock. She couldn't wait to get in it. Nothing but a bit of fabric to stop stuff biting you and touching you. Ugh!!!

Might see more orangutans. Rendy said there's a female with a baby nearby. They sometimes get curious when the camp is busy. Could see them any time :) Baby orangutans are the cutest!!!

He smelled hot, but the young males reminded me of my year 9's. All swagger and show. Into the trees with a mouthful of food before a real adult turns up! Rather have a classroom of young orangutans TBH! Rendy said have to be careful of full adult males. Women smell the same as a female orangutan if you're having your period. I know how I feel about that and I don't think he'd like it! […]

Rendy's a quiet stud. Maybe I should go back to uni and do anthropology. Find a sexy researcher in the jungle. Wouldn't mind getting hot and sweaty then, haha. […]

Think this place is making me more horny. Don't laugh it's possible. Everything's green and alive. No pollution. Air's clean like Macchu Picchu but thick and warm like Vietnam. I do want to enjoy this experience and I know I'm lucky to be here.

Might have a cold shower to wake me up. Breakfast time soon. 7am it's not exactly a holiday is it? Think I can hear someone sweeping outside. Do these Indonesians never sleep?

Sleepless 4 u. Ali xx

---

[4] Insect repellent

Diary: Harriet Kelley, evening

```
Harriet Kelley uses an expensive lilac Moleskine
diary, writing in a neat 'cursive' style common to
well-educated Americans. I have only included a few
excerpts here, but she writes extensively about her
delight at being in the rainforest and the wonder
of seeing orangutans and other wildlife, although
she clearly had mixed feelings about the privations
of camp life.
```

Well, Harriet, you said you wanted some hard work this summer. They weren't joking about physical labour. You'll be shopping a size or more down when you get home if it's like this all the way through.

At least you can have a shower at the end of the day here, or twice a day if you need to. They call it a shower. I call it a bucket of cold water filled from a hose, but I wouldn't want hot water here anyways. And the showers are private — Tara says last year they were pretty much communal and open air.

I was sweating like a racehorse after we tore out the wallboards this morning and pulled up half the floor this afternoon. It wasn't a moment too soon after poor Alison almost fell through that hole last night.

Anyhow it's just a shell now, all posts and window frames with half a floor. I'm stunned how we did so much with just pointing and saying a few words of English and Indonesian. They don't speak much English apart from Rendy, the camp manager, and Dewi, his assistant. He's a charming young man, so intelligent and polite and passionate about the rainforest and the wildlife, and she's just like a little version of him, quite pretty underneath that headscarf. I can see she adores him even if he don't notice.

They're like a little family, though Bimo sometimes looks at Dewi like she's a goat in a flock of sheep. He's grumpy as a mule anyway, never talks to anyone except Revo and Ibu Intan, the cook. I wish I could talk to her better. I bet we'd have a few stories to share over the fire. I'm on kitchen duty in a few days' time so I'll try to get to know her then. I'd love to get a few tips on her cooking — she cooks up a mess in the jungle that puts my cowgirl pot-wrangling skills to shame. I don't think any of us could eat enough at lunch or dinner after a days' work, but I don't think we'll starve here! Where it all comes from is a mystery.

Everyone has gotten to know each other a bit more today. We all talked on the boat yesterday, but the walls between folks fall down fast when you've spent all day handing each other crowbars and chisels and puzzling together over some task the locals probably do without a thought. I ended up laughing so hard with Maya when we were both trying to saw through a piece of wood this afternoon. I don't think either of us have ever sawed anything tougher than a loaf of bread. That idiot Cristian was showing off, boasting how he could saw through a piece of wood on his own, and I just said "you'll cut your fingers off if you don't look at the wood instead of your guns". He's all big hat and no cattle. Maya started giggling and then she saw how bad our wood looked, and before you know it we were both cackling. She's alright, that girl. I remember what it's like to be young and she's just having fun. I'd have been spanked for flirting in public with a boy when I was her age. And a boy like Cristian? My daddy woulda tanned his ass for looking at me!

We all want this place to be happy, so I'll hold fire unless he properly steps over the line. So long as he doesn't do anything Maya doesn't want, and they take it somewhere else. They mostly just talk crap about kids' TV from the 90s and pop music, and she pulls silly poses for him to photograph.

Paul's a cool glass of water on a hot day. I thought I'd frightened him off when I hugged him at the airport, but he's a very sweet man, and he watches everyone around him. He made me chuckle tonight with little remarks about everyone. It's a shame he likes men, but all the best ones do. He gets on with Alison, too. Well, they're teachers so why wouldn't he? But she's not what I expected. Much more shy than the experienced traveller who answered my questions in our Facebook group. Doesn't give up much about her home life, either. She didn't look like she'd slept a wink last night. Maybe it's just jet-lag and the heat.

I hope Tara doesn't get too bothered by my snoring again tonight. I don't want to get on the wrong side of the woman in charge of us, but she is my roomie. It's just who I am.

They're fixing to take us on a night walk into the rainforest. There's a path through the jungle and we might see all kinds of strange animals in the dark, but we can only go on it with a guide.

***

WOAH! That was incredible! Birds and bats and spiders everywhere! Rendy and Dewi and Revo and Bimo were just pointing at things in the darkness and then — whoosh! — there was a tree-rat or a bird or something. I saw Bimo smile for the first time. He loves spiders! Alison wasn't happy about them but I loved them too.

I could have cheerfully shoved that fool Cristian's face into a tarantula's nest. Who uses a camera flash on a night walk? Just stop horn-dogging for one god-damn minute! And Maya, I know they say pretty girls make fools, but this one's fool enough already.

Horny kids aside, it was like being in one of those PBS documentaries with that posh Brit. I can handle the sweaty days if we get a few more safaris like that. Tara said that in a few days we'll go some place where they feed rescued orangutans after they release them into the wild, and maybe a boat trip at sundown.

Diary: Dewi Rifqi, night

How exciting it is to see the camp full of people, and to have Rendy back again. Tara is exactly as I would want to be. She is independent and strong. She has her own business. I think Rendy would notice me as a woman if I was more like her and could go where I want to go when I want to go there. He still looks at me like a girl or a student. She is very nice and she wanted to know all about me, where I am from and why I want to help the wildlife. It was almost like meeting the Founder again, but I was a lot less nervous! She worked very hard today — they all worked very hard — and it was like she was at home, building her own house. I think it makes her very happy to be here. Harriet reminds me of my aunt, who told my father that I should go to university if I wanted to do it and dared him to say no. Alison did not look happy today, but I remember my first night in the rainforest and I hope she will get used to it as I did. I cannot imagine sleeping now without the noise of the animals outside. Maya is very pretty and full of life. I think she would take off her overshirt straight away if there were no men here, or even if only Bimo was not here. She is the same age as I am, and I wonder if all women of my age are so free and full of confidence where she is from? I hope we can be friends.

Paul is a nice man, but he is not like the other men here. Very quiet and thoughtful and gentle, and not at all muscular. I suppose he is a little bit like Rendy but there is something else, perhaps because he talks to the women without looking at their bodies at all, like other women do. He must love his wife very much.

I do not like Cristian. He is handsome and strong I suppose, but he is very crude and I do not like the way he looks at Maya, like he is a cat and she is a piece of meat. Sometimes he looks at

Alison the same way, but not Tara. If he looked at me that way I would not feel safe. But sometimes Maya and Alison look at him in the same way too, and I think about Rendy. There are times when I find myself staring at him while he works. Am I looking at him that way?

Rendy led everyone into the forest tonight as a reward for working so hard. We showed them the birdwatching tower they can visit, and the forbidden path where we keep the camera traps, and then we pointed out the night-time animals that you can only see when you know what to look for. I like the night-walks because we become a team. Even Bimo looks happy when he is pointing out things. We would probably have seen more if Alison had not squealed quite so loudly when he made the very large tarantula come out of its hole. I know he only does it as a test to see who he can scare, I wanted to scream so much when I saw it, but he reminds me of my father and I did not want to let them think that I was too scared to stay in the rainforest.

Instagram: Cristian Jarvis

```
Cristian's  next  picture  looks  like  playful
flirtation  as  Maya  blows  him  a  kiss,  dressed in
pyjamas  at  the  door  of  her  bedroom.  The  caption
suggests  his  relationship  with  Maya  had  become
physical, if not sexual.
```

@pecstourist Jungle hottie Maya can play the innocent all she wants. Those aren't stage kisses she's blowing. They won't be all she's blowing soon 🍆 💦 😉.

#itstartswithakiss #notsoinnocent #nightwalk #outofsight #playtime #givingitup #stepbystep #shewantsitall

Email: Alan Caudwell to Imogen Nicholson

To: founder@saveorangutans.org.uk
From: alan@caudwell.org.uk
Subject: Pondok Bahaya diaries - July 25
Date: 27 August 2018 09:02

Jenny,

Glad to hear you've found someone to handle the PR nightmare. It will be wonderful to catch up, although I don't think you'll find any more peace here than you have in the UK.

I saw that some of the families want to come out here to put pressure on the Indonesian authorities to tell them what they've found at PB. I can't imagine that it will do anything except bring more press over from the UK with them — or even worse it will bring the US media for that Texan woman. It's not like they'll be able to sneak in — the river's the only way to get there.

I see Cristian's still the demon of the month: that woman from Thailand that he met on a conservation project, spilling the beans about his tastes for drugs, violent sex and prostitutes. He sounds like a charming shit, but aren't the worst of them always like that? Whatever happened here, I think he'll be in the thick of it.

I'd like to know what the camp looked like when they found it. I remember the layout from my visit a few years ago, and I still have the photos, but I'd like to speak to the OST guys who got there first. Pak Rafi says the OST offices are still under siege. If I go there, someone might connect me to you. It wouldn't be hard to join the dots. He's offered to arrange a meeting with your men, if they're happy to do it and you are. I got the impression that they're still in shock.

Alan x

Thursday, July 26, 2018

Camera traps

Dewi is responsible for setting up and monitoring camera traps around Pondok Bahaya. These small units are strapped to trees, equipped with motion detectors and a night-vision camera. An infrared lamp illuminates the area in front of the camera, which can be set to take either photos or video. Dewi's duties include swapping the memory cards and copying the data every few days. She had made her rounds until about a week after the volunteers arrived, but it looked like there was a backlog of files to review, and the latest data had not been checked.

The cameras were kept away from the main path which circled through the rainforest near Pondok Bahaya, and although I had no idea exactly where Alison had roamed, I hoped she might have been captured. What I found on the night of Alison's first walk was quite unexpected.

Dewi carefully logged the camera locations with GPS, and this image comes from an outlying camera

```
about three kilometres north of the camp. The
distance is hard to judge, but a figure appears at
the limit of the camera's night vision. There is no
mistaking an elderly man, his back bent, wearing a
long loincloth that hangs to the ground. He walks
across the field of view, and his face is turned
away from the camera. No-one from the OST
recognises this man, and he bears no resemblance to
any of the staff or volunteers.
```

Diary: Tara Fowler, evening

Back to work! The group has thrown themselves into the programme, and we had the walls off the old building in no time at all. Rendy had the group chiselling joints to repair the frame today, with mixed success. The rest of us were either pulling old nails out of the frame or levering up the floorboards. I'd forgotten how hard it is, but it feels great! I'll sleep like a log tonight.

The accommodation is a lot more pleasant than last year. No-one feels great with rats running around and the stress of having to shit through a hole over the river. Here's to actual bunk beds and a toilet block with a door and a shower!!! This place feels like the Ritz to me! It's probably the hardest thing the other volunteers have ever done, but this should be an easy month if everyone settles in and gets on.

Rendy seems more relaxed, and that might be down to having an assistant to help out with some of the organisation and keep up with the conservation work while we're here. He says there's a lot of wildlife in the forest around the camp, but he doesn't usually leave the camera traps running while we're here because he doesn't have time to check them when the memory cards fill up. This time he has an assistant checking them so we might see some really new footage of a clouded leopard[5], or tarsiers[6] or orangutans. Everyone was full of energy after seeing the orangutans feeding on the way here, so anything like that will help them to keep their spirits up when it starts to get tough in a couple of weeks. Dewi is only a post-graduate student but she is very friendly, clever and grown-up — she makes Maya and Cristian look like a couple of teenagers.

Talking of immature people, Cristian keeps interrupting their work to take photos of her, and I think she can't stop herself pulling more and more ridiculous poses. It was funny at the start, but after two days it's getting tired. And some of her poses are a bit too, well, sexy, for the Indonesians. And for the rest of us, to be honest. So after dinner tonight, I decided to tell the volunteers about Anthony and Clare, the two volunteers who had an affair when I was on my first trip. I know the punchline is Clare's boyfriend surprising her at the airport in Jakarta and proposing in front of Anthony, but the point was that they had been sneaking away from the camp with a blanket and a couple of sleeping bags to get together AWAY from everyone else. We all knew about it, but the rumour — because Anthony told one of the other men — was that Clare sounded like an angry macaque when they were at it.

I know it was clumsy, and Maya looked furious, but I think she got the point. I'm not sure Cristian got it, he just looked a bit smug, but it takes two, right? I didn't feel I had any choice after Harriet went to call them back up from the dock after lunch today and she had a face like a dog chewing a wasp. She said nothing had happened, but any of the Indonesians could have walked down

---

[5] The clouded leopard is a medium-sized cat, more at home in the trees than on the ground, noted for its long tail and black ring markings.
[6] A tarsier is a small nocturnal primate, known for its very large eyes and long feet, and for being very difficult to observe.

there. Holding hands in public is as far as it goes here, and if they were copping off…FFS! Dewi was a bit shocked by the story, I think, but Rendy will explain it to her later. I guess she's probably a bit more innocent than Maya.

So what else has gone on since we got here? I got my hammock out to sleep in the open like last year. Harriet snores like an elephant so I didn't wait. I don't mean that because she's big, but I like my sleep and I've never had trouble sleeping here, not like Alison. The jungle is noisy, but after a while it's just like white noise. Last year I couldn't sleep when I got home because it was so quiet! Alison's suffering though, even with earplugs. I hope she'll just get so tired she starts to pass out and then she'll get used to it when she's decided the forest isn't full of monsters waiting to get her, but she does get more than her fair share of mozzie bites and she was freaked out by the spiders last night, so maybe it is full of monsters trying to get HER.

Oh yeah! Everyone got a crash course in Indonesian this morning from Rendy and Dewi. No-one's bothered to learn any before they came here of course, and I'm just starting to remember everything I've forgotten since last year. I wonder how long it will take for one of them to work out that Pondok Bahaya means 'Camp Danger'. I know it's got something to do with an old indigenous folk name for this area, but it's a stupid name if you ask me — it won't help Alison.

Diary: Dewi Rifqi, evening

These volunteers are full of surprises. I know that sounds like my mother and father telling me to be careful of Western people with their lax morals, but I did not think Tara would tell a story about people having sex, not in front of the whole group. And they laughed at the end when the boyfriend of the woman proposed to her in front of the man she had been sleeping with. It was like the Korean soap operas my grandmother watches. Rendy explained later that it was a warning to Maya and Cristian. Tara was concerned that they would start kissing on the dock or have sex in one of the rooms. I would not like that but Bimo and Ibu Intan would be very angry. Maya went bright red — I have never seen anyone blush that colour before. Cristian just smiled like a little boy. He is like the bad boys my mother told me to stay away from.

And they have not bothered to learn any Indonesian. I have been learning English since I was a little girl, and Revo knows a little, but Bimo and Ibu Intan only speak Indonesian Bahasa and Dayak[7]. Rendy said that because the English used to rule the world, they do not think they should have to speak any other languages and everyone else should learn English. So today we taught them some basic Indonesian like hello, please and thank you. And we reminded them of our names again. I was surprised that Maya of all people remembered the most words and started asking Rangga and Revo for the names of things, but Paul was trying hard. Harriet said she would try but her head is too full to learn new words. She is American, so I suppose it is different for her anyway. And she talks a lot so it might be hard for her to hear other people. Oh, that is rude :)

Tara said she will remember all of her Indonesian words in a few days. I do not know what to make of her. She is very close to Rendy, I can see that, but I do not know if it is just friendship or something more. It would be strange after the warning she gave to Maya and Cristian. They are supposed to send home anyone who has a romantic relationship with an Indonesian, but I suppose they cannot send themselves home. Anyway, it may be just my heart making me jealous. I know that in England it is perfectly normal

---

[7] The Dayak are the native people of Borneo. There are more than 200 Dayak groups, with their own dialects, customs, laws, territory and culture.

for men and women to have close friendships with nothing intimate happening between them, but here everybody just assumes the worst. I should learn to be more tolerant. They are just friends I am sure. But what if they are not? Maybe Tara was talking to me as well as to Maya and Cristian? I would not sleep with a man before marriage, but she does not know that. It is too confusing.

I should be more concerned about Alison than about myself or Tara and Cristian. I do not think that she has slept since she arrived. She looks so tired. I am worried that she will hurt herself or become ill if she does not rest soon.

Instagram: Cristian Jarvis

Cristian's confidence with Maya reaches its peak in this photo. They're at the end of the jetty, one of the more private locations in Camp Bahaya. Although she's wearing long loose trousers, she's lying back on the dock and has daringly removed her shirt from over a tight vest-top, which is now rolled up to expose her belly, while blowing a kiss at the camera (and the photographer, one assumes).

The light suggests that it's the middle of the day. Was this the scene Harriet found when she went to call Maya and Cristian back to work before Tara gave them her thinly-veiled warning?

@Pecstourist Need to find a jungle gym for @maya to play in 🌴 🐒

🍌 🐵 🦎 #hotinthejungle #readytopluck #bitchinheat #playtime

Diary: Maya Pollard

Maya's diary, bought from Paperchase, had a bright plastic cover of tropical leaves, parrots and monkeys. She writes with a neat but simple joined-up script that's easy to read and fills each line.

Her diary began on Monday, July 23rd, rueing the lack of outside communication but largely positive about her fellow volunteers and excited about the basic nature of the camp, although she didn't enjoy her first cold shower. Like the others, she was exhausted by her first two days of hard work in the tropical heat and humidity.

It is interesting to note that while everyone else was talking about her flirtation with Cristian Jarvis, she had not mentioned him again after briefly describing him as "hench, hot and funny AF" on the first day.

I will not be labelled the camp whore. People can be so judgmental. All I wanted to do was flirt with Cris for a few weeks, and Tara acts like we were going to have sex in front of everyone by the end of the first week. I know he's a bit full-on, but it's 2018 and if a woman can't flirt with a man in public then I might as well wear a headscarf and moon around after a man like soppy Dewi. So obvs she likes Rendy. How do men never see it?

So anyway now it's a thing with everyone there's no point flirting. If I had sex with Cris — if I even let him think I was that easy — everyone will know and fucking Tara will be right and I'm not giving her the satisfaction of calling me out. TBH it was fun kissing him last night a bit but he was all over me down the dock today and I'm sure he thinks I'm desperate to jump him as soon as. That was never my plan. And the fucking arsehole just looked like he was going to laugh when I was going bright red and I'm definitely not going to fuck a guy who won't stand up for me in public.

I tried to tell Alison but it's like talking to a fucking zombie. I suppose I should be thankful I can sleep here. If she's not complaining about how she can't sleep she's going on about the fucking mosquitoes, and I know they are bad, but we all have to put up with them and she's put so much deet on her that it can't be healthy. That's probably what's keeping her awake all night.

I wouldn't mind being able to take off a few layers. Forget about showing off to Cris or anyone else, I just want to feel a breeze and some sunshine on my back. At night you have to wear long sleeves and trousers and sleep in pyjamas in case something gets through your mozzie net, and in the day you have to wear long sleeves and trousers because the Indonesians will throw us in the river with the crocs or burn us for witches or something retarded. It's not fucking fair. The men all walk down to the river and take their clothes off and jump in as soon as we've finished work, and I can't even do a bit of sunbathing. WTAF is that about?!

I can't believe they'd do anything bad to us. I know Bimo's a bit scowly but Revo's funny AF and he's always laughing with Ibu Intan. Rendy's always chatting and Dewi seems lovely too. How could I offend them?

And Rangga's got some muscles on him. Hard not to notice. And not like the gym muscles Cris has got. He's got a sweet smile, too. When things calm down it would be nice to make a new friend. Just a friend, though.

Letter: Alison Pierce to Manny James

Mannylicious,

It's official: I am not a jungle kind of girl. Party girl, beach girl, mountain trekking girl. Not a jungle girl. You're right. I will pay my penance 😵 […]

Jungle sounds no better than my voices. A noise that won't go away. Screeching and buzzing all day and all night. Louder at night because there's nothing making a noise. Tried earplugs and listening to music. Nothing blocks it out. Music helps but battery in my phone won't last a whole night. Hard to charge it with the generator just running in the evening. Wish I had one of those solar chargers.

Have to listen to Maya instead. Lots of noise tonight lol Her flirting with Cris might be over. Lol lol

Everyone shocked tonight after dinner. Tara talked about the two volunteers having an affair last year. Kissing in public. Rules here very strict about relationships with locals. Didn't think they might be offended by us making out in public. It's not Ayia Napa though. Guess it would be pretty rude. Have to be extra careful.

Maya was pissed off. What did she expect? Flirts all day with Cris. They went down to the dock at lunchtime. No-one wanted to check on them in case it started a problem. Harriet went down to call them back to work. She didn't seem too pleased. That jetty is way too public.

Found Maya in my bunk. Face down on the pillow. Heard her crying. Wanted my bed back so had to ask if she was OK. Also good person sometimes 😏

Started telling me she was just having fun. Didn't mean it to go anywhere. Everyone thinks she's a slut. Nah babe, I thought. I slut for England. You're amateur.

Then the juicy bit. She snogged him last night and a bit today. Down on the dock. Today he got hands-on. She pulled back before Harriet came down. She really wasn't going to fuck him. She'll cool it off now. Hang out with the rest of us more. Great news for all! Tried not to look more pleased. Might tell Tara. Keep it confidential but she'll be relieved. Everything will be more relaxed.

So me and Maya we're girl buddies now. Told me about her clingy boyfriend at uni. She thinks Cris groping her tits when they snog is hardcore. Didn't tell her what I do with you at weekends. And weeknights. Might blow her mind. [...]

Cris's free now if I want. I really do. He's a dickhead but I'm not interested in the head!!!

Don't think I'll have to wait long. We were both brushing our teeth tonight. Not a sexy moment but no one else was around. Was stretching my shoulders from today's hammering. Cristian made a show of stretching himself. Said we should do some yoga before we start work tomorrow. Says he did it every morning in Thailand. Should tell him about my morning stretches in Thailand. Remember that? Probably bullshit but he spent plenty of time watching me stretch. Appreciate the balls on a man playing for two women so shamelessly. […] Doesn't even know one of them's dumping him. I said yes. Of course. Love a stupid holiday hunk.

Need to think of places to take him. The showers? That rickety birdwatching tower? Nothing like a bit of danger! […]

Already know I won't sleep tonight. Too noisy. Too horny. Might go for a walk. Fuck the spookiness. See if I can find anywhere for some fun. Might have some on my own. Wrap up against the mozzies. Put on my big shoes. Got to be better than going mad awake in bed.

Sniff these sticky fingerprints babe. Ali xx

Email: Imogen Nicholson to Alan Caudwell

To: alan@caudwell.org.uk
From: founder@saveorangutans.org.uk
Subject: Re: Pondok Bahaya diaries - July 26
Date: 28 August 2018 07:11

Alan,

Keep the diaries coming. By the time the next batch reaches me I may well be knocking on your door, if I can evade the press when I land at Jakarta and PKB.

Your second prediction came true this morning, although I'm hardly surprised to hear that Alison had an active sex life. Okay, that's putting it mildly, and I know she was a teacher, but compared to Cristian she was just having a lot of good times. She kept it completely separate from her job, her parents didn't know about it, and it doesn't sound like anyone did anything they didn't want to do, but I bet that she'll be treated far worse than him. All those photos and videos that have been leaked from that adult dating website — and I've only seen the censored pictures that have been in the newspapers.

Her diaries make a lot more sense to me now. No wonder she was frustrated that Cristian didn't go for her. She must have felt like she was in a desert with no water and there was a hosepipe being dangled in front of her!

The figure in the camera trap video is a mystery to me. His clothing reminds me of the Dayak, one of the indigenous groups in Kalimantan. They are nomadic, but there are no Dayak sites in the OST's forest reserve, and I don't believe that they would disrespect our boundaries.

We should discuss it with Pak Rafi when I arrive.

Jenny x

Friday, July 27, 2018

Photos: Cristian

Like Alison, Cristian is a light sleeper, but he takes advantage of either insomnia or an excess of energy to look for real wildlife. Paul must be a heavy sleeper, because his room-mate is out every night. The results are grainy, wide shots designed to soak up as much light as possible. Only those at short range, of cooperative insects and birds, have very much detail, although sometimes he takes several shots together. I've looked up some techniques for night photography, and concluded that he's planning to combine them together later to get a better image. He must be using a small tripod to keep the camera steady.

On the fourth night, a figure appears in Cristian's photos. They're seen initially from the top of the birdwatching tower, a few hundred metres inland and uphill from the main camp, and he follows them into the forest. The images are noisy and the figure is small and indistinct at first, but the hair, build and loose clothing strongly suggest it's Alison. There's no evidence from the diaries that anyone else is taking late night strolls on their own.

Cristian must be stealthy to follow her undetected. There are several photos, taken across a couple of hours, and he continues to photograph animals and insects as he follows her around. It's not clear whether she returns to the camp as he follows her, or if he gets bored or tired and returns on his own timetable.

Cristian's expensive camera also tags each image with a GPS location. It will be possible to map where both he and Alison wander on their nocturnal treks.

Camera traps

The old man appears again on a video trap, much closer to the camp than the previous night. He is slumped against a tree, facing the camera, his eyes glazed and apparently unaware that he's being recorded. The IR light washes out his features, but he's clearly indigenous to Borneo and not from Java.

Faded tattoos cover much of his body, with triangles around the neck, sweeping curves like flowers and vines — or snakes and tentacles, and wild, laughing, toothed faces. His earlobes dangle almost to his shoulders, with sagging holes in them where they have been pierced and stretched for many years.

Within half an hour, and only about 500 metres south of where the unidentified man is resting, Alison walks slowly past a camera, her feet brushing through the leaves and forest litter but rising to avoid rocks and logs even though her gaze wanders absent-mindedly around the jungle. She is in an area that's off-limits to anyone except the

```
staff, a dreamlike expression on her face. The
camera catches the glare of her head-torch from
about 10 metres away, but she doesn't appear to
notice it.
```

Diary: Tara Fowler, morning

Finally! It looks like the story last night worked. The whole Maya/Cristian thing seems to be cooling off. Alison took me to one side after breakfast and said that Maya was incredibly embarrassed, she was only having fun with Cristian but she didn't mean to offend anyone. I don't know if that's true, but she did seem to be a bit cooler towards Cristian this morning so fingers crossed. I'm not sure Cristian has got the message yet — hopefully she's explaining it to him at lunchtime while I'm writing this. I'll speak to Rendy so he can tell Bimo to calm down.

Now all I need to do is find a way to help Alison sleep and we can all enjoy being here. That woman looks so tired. It's like she's got Tescos bags under her eyes. She's on kitchen duty so I'll tell her to just have a lie down this afternoon after the washing up. Maybe she can get some rest. The noise isn't as noticeable in the daytime anyway.

It's such a shame, because everyone else is getting on well and we're making good progress. Harriet and Paul just chat away and laugh like old friends, and even Cristian works hard when he's not flirting or showing off. He can put those muscles to work when he wants to. The rate he's going, he'll have the rest of the floorboards out of the hall by the end of the day.

And the hammock. So good to be wrapped up in my little cocoon at night, nodding off with the jungle around me and waking up with the sun. Not much wakes me when I'm out in that thing, but this morning I woke up with the feeling that someone had been hanging around in the night. HA! Hanging around a hammock!

Sounds like the sort of silly joke that would keep Maya and Cristian cracked up for hours.

But seriously, it was creepy.

Diary: Maya, afternoon

Insane day, man! I decided to play it cool with Cris this morning and hoped he'd get the message. We can still have bants and a laugh, right, I thought? Turns out old Cris isn't as smart as he is good lookin, in fact he's a bit of a fucking idiot. He just looked a bit confused when I didn't flirt back this morning, none of the stupid high-fives and air-kisses we've been doing for days. I kind of missed it but I was like, Maya, play it cool girl.

So he's trying to make flirty dirty jokes all morning even when I was working on the other side of the building to get some space, so after lunch I took him down to the jetty and told him what's what. He seemed cool, but he was all, 'keep it on the low down, gotcha Maya'. Whatever. It's cool, I thought. He gets it. Turns out he did not get it.

I was chatting to Harriet and Tara and trying to pick up some of the old lingo from Rendy and from nowhere Cris grabbed me by the TITS and he's like grinding his hips into my arse in some insane rhythm in his head.

I do not know what noise came out of me but Tara goes apeshit at Cris while I'm trying to get his hands off me. She's screaming at him the thing I told Alison which I thought was just between us. I'm just getting flashbacks to that time when I was 16 on the way home from school and that's some therapy shit I don't want to go back to. All I can hear is people yelling and then Bimo's laughing at Cris so now it turns out everyone knows I've gone cool on him and that's not cool it's between the two of us. Cris looks like he's going to take on Bimo, but sometimes that guy looks fucking hardcore like he could kill a man for shits and giggles. They start to face off and then Rangga is just there, like totally strong and invincible even though he's a foot smaller than Cris, and he just sends Cris to his room like a little kid.

And then Harriet has my hand and takes me down to the dock and I'm telling her things I don't want to talk about, but she's just nodding and listening and I let it all out and I'm sorry if I was annoying people but I thought he was cool and he's a dick and then Tara's there and Harriet's chilling her out too. I know Cris wasn't going to do anything but just for a minute there it was too scary. What an asshat.

FFS, I need to stop writing like a kid. If anyone ever reads this they're going to think I'm such a retard. Deep breath, girl. Don't wake Alison — I think she's asleep. Miracle.

Diary: Paul, night

Well who would have thought the drama could get better? Tara pulled a master stroke last night with her story about the perils of jungle affairs, and this morning it looked like Maya has decided to cool things down with Cristian. The only problem was that she hadn't told Cristian he was in the refrigerator and he thought she was playing hard to get or some stupid game. So we had a quiet morning just getting on with stuff and watching some monkeys go through the trees near the river, and they went down to the jetty after lunch, when Alison decides to tell Harriet and I about her chat with Maya the night before. The one that was apparently in confidence, although I don't think Alison knows what she's saying half the time at the moment, the poor girl. Who else has she told, I wondered? I was about to find out.

I thought those years were behind me, but when your CV says 'headteacher for 12 years', people expect that you will know how to deal with this kind of situation. I suppose there was no-one else to talk to young Cristian after he embarrassed himself. Alison is in no place to offer sound advice at the moment, poor girl. I told them to give him half an hour to calm down and I'd go over with a cup of tea, which was really giving myself enough time to break out a soothing bag of camomile.

I must give credit to Harriet. She brought Maya and Tara back up from the river with smiles on their faces, and she seemed to know that I had agreed to talk to Cristian. Or she'd volunteered me. Who needs enemies, eh?

Cristian was listening to music when I took him a cup of tea (builder's only for that boy). He greeted me with a mix of anger and fear that I have seen many times in young men who have embarrassed themselves in public and realised the consequences are real. Cristian's not that young, but I don't think he's ever grown up. I've heard it all before, how he got carried away having a bit of fun with Maya but he didn't know she would be upset or that Bimo would be so offended.

In a school that would have been a sexual assault — it WAS a sexual assault, there's no question about it. He needs to grow up fast. I laid it out for him in simple terms and he seemed to understand that what he did was very wrong.

Then came the blame: Tara for being a 'frigid ugly bitch' who was sticking her nose in a bit of fun that was none of her business, and Bimo and the 'fucking Indonesians' for being so sensitive. And what would they do if they knew I was gay? Trying to keep my temper, I suggested that so long as I keep my sexuality to myself it's none of their business, and none of his, either.

And finally the sob story — literally with tears — that this was his last chance to do something good and prove to his father that he's not a surfer who bums around the world getting into trouble with women and getting bailed out. Where does his father think he got it all from, anyway? And so on…I tried not to ask but these things always tumble out once you open the floodgates. Father's a dirty old bastard, Cristian has a successful older brother, wanted to be an environmental lawyer but spent too much time partying to get a good degree.

I was thinking about a second cup of tea when he got to the pregnant girlfriend his father is paying for, and the gap year he took to get away from it all. The gap year that has been going on for five years. Joining this project is his way to reconnect with his ambition to help the environment, but he can't help himself with women. If you ask me, Maya has had a lucky escape. She's a young woman with prospects; he's an erection attached to a wounded ego.

When he had let it all out I said what I always tell them: you will get a second chance — only one — if you apologise to everyone and change your behaviour. Not, as I wanted to say: stop blaming everyone else and start swimming now because they shouldn't have to waste fuel taking you back when you do something else stupid. He looked at me very earnestly, thanked me, and said he would think about it. Sometimes boys like Cristian simply learn to appear contrite. Only time will tell.

Diary: Maya, night

I helped in the kitchen this afternoon. Ibu Intan doesn't speak any English but she's nice all the same. It's just chop this, chop that, stir this, put this flavour in. I'm not a big cook at home or uni but she makes you feel like you've made huge pots of tasty food, and the thing is, it IS tasty even though it's just stir-fried vegetables with fried noodles and like a bottomless pot of rice. I was pretty hungry after all that intense shit this afternoon but there's always enough for seconds. Can't fault it. We're a long way from KFC but it helped me to chill out.

I think everyone just wanted to get to bedtime with no more dramas. Can't argue with that. Alison looked better than she has since we got here, and if Cris had stayed in his room that would have been fine. I know Paul had talked to him but I didn't know what was going to happen when he walked out of that room. Was he going to just self-destruct in front of us? It was edgy AF and I was a relieved when he said sorry. More than anything else.

So fair's fair but I wasn't going to stand up and applaud. That was some backwards shit he pulled.

But then it's on me to accept it? Everyone was looking at me, waiting for me to let him off the hook. Tara and Rendy want to get out of a shit decision. I don't want to go home early any more than anyone else does. I don't want the orangutan people who brought us here to get into trouble.

So what kind of cutting acceptance did I come up with to put him in his place, me with my four A's and my first-class degree in progress?

"Yeah, OK, don't do it again. You're an idiot." FML. At least everyone else started breathing again.

Apology or not, I half expected Bimo would have put him in the river, so full credit to Rangga for owning that moment. Honestly he's a bit of a god to me right now. I just thought he was a carpenter.

Diary: Rendy, night

I must thank Rangga for his help today. Without his quick thinking, I would be sending someone home or even to the hospital. I know that Cristian behaved inappropriately towards Maya, but Bimo must control his anger. I know that he loves the forest and I often feel safer knowing that he is here when there are illegal miners upriver and illegal loggers could be in the forest. All the same, he is too easy to provoke. Sometimes I think he wants to be provoked to let something out. Something that is not good.

I know that I have his respect as the manager of this camp, and we have often talked about what the forest means to him, but I do not feel that he always respects me as a man. I know that I am the outsider, the educated manager from Java come to save the rainforest from ignorant Kalimantan locals. I am a 30-year-old man without a wife or children, and that is unusual here. Rangga is all of the things I am not, and it is clear that Bimo respects him in a different way.

As for Cristian, I hope that his apology is genuine. Tara believes that we should give him the opportunity to prove it. I admire her generosity. He is a strong worker and I would not like to lose him, so I will follow her judgement.

It is Tara's own problems which worry me this evening. I would not have found this out for several weeks, perhaps, if today had not been so full of drama. When she returned from the dock with Maya and it seemed that the crisis had passed, I thought it would be a good idea to walk along the forest paths and talk about our options. I observed that she seemed unhappy but I did not wish to intrude. I believe that she had been waiting for me to ask about it for some days.

Her business partner, to whom she was engaged, had been dishonest with her and run up debts for gambling and other expenses. He had concealed them from her and had used their shared funds to pay them off. She discovered the problem shortly after her return from the last conservation project and he blamed her for his behaviour, tried to turn their mutual friends against her, was verbally abusive to her and her family, and even to her employees. The distraction caused problems with her work, and she eventually separated from him and had to buy him out of her life so that he could pay his debts and leave the area. Even now, he often sends her abusive messages.

What I would do to this man does not bear writing down in case I incriminate myself in future. I would welcome and cherish a woman of her strength, character and beauty in my life, and perhaps impulsively I told her this. She was quiet for some time before she told me that it was too soon for her to consider another attachment, and that she values my friendship too highly to change it to something else. There is also the matter of our professional relationship, and the strict rules the charity has expressed, forbidding intimate relationships between staff and volunteers. I apologised for being unprofessional in expressing my feelings. Tara said she was very flattered. I promised to respect the feelings of my friend and support her.

Perhaps Dewi will be able to offer me some advice on how to proceed.

Letter: Alison Pierce to Manny James

Mannymannymanny,

You know how sex is the only thing that stops my night voices? All my thoughts screaming like a class-full of 13-year-olds after their mid-morning sugar fix. Might have found something else. You know what that means to me. Only you know. Wish you were here to tell. […]

Don't worry babe. I'll still fuck you for the tingles but last night I found peace out here. I went outside for a walk.

Sounds crazy, yeah? It's not I swear. Felt like I was floating. The jungle wasn't noisy any more. It sang a lullaby in my head.

Went out looking for places to hook up with Cris. Pretended to be sleeping until Maya was asleep with her headphones on. Heard the Indonesians go to bed. Wrapped up so the mozzies couldn't bite. Red light on my torch shows me everything. Spider eyes everywhere like fairy lights. Birds and little deer. Not too many creepy crawly things on the path.

Didn't even notice the time go. Like my brain slowed down. Just the jungle noise in my head. Then I was back into the camp. Nearly bumped into the old lady making breakfast. Don't think she saw me. Wonder if she even is an old lady? Bet this place makes you grow old fast.

Still horny as fuck though babe. My secret hunger. You're the first man who was cool with it. Even before I landed on my head. Always answer my booty call. Don't mind if I find someone else. Always poking me in the back when I wake up. Can't say no to you. […]

Have to let Cris fill your spot for now. Or mine lol. Maya's a little tease. I'd never say no to all that beef. Warned off by head girl Tara. And the drama today!!! All cock no brains. Fine. I don't need brains.

Last night's a bit vague though. Think I found somewhere to take Cris. Have to make sure Tara doesn't make us cool it down. Doing her a favour if I calm him down. Have another look tonight. Jungle's looking good to me now. […]

Have you fucked anyone yet? It's been a week since I left. I thought of you on a hook-up date. Meeting a stranger. I like to watch you in my head with other girls. One of us should be getting some.

Hot in the jungle, Ali xxxx

Email: Alan Caudwell to Imogen Nicholson

To: founder@saveorangutans.org.uk
From: alan@caudwell.org.uk
Subject: Pondok Bahaya diaries - July 27
Date: 29 August 2018 09:22

Jenny,

It will be great to see you. I hope you have time to read the latest entries when you have settled in.

Cristian's photos and the camera trap images have started to tell me their own story. I'm starting to think that this old man wandering through the forest near Pondok Bahaya is not there by accident. He looks very frail, but every day brings him closer to your camp, and every night he is more likely to cross paths with either Alison or Cristian.

I hope the latest revelations about Alison don't tarnish the OST's reputation. It looks like she wants to have sex at every photogenic tourist hotspot in the world. You have to admire someone who takes photos like that in Macchu Picchu, Angkor Wat and Stonehenge. I mean, Stonehenge? Surely someone noticed! And Macchu Picchu? I could hardly breathe after climbing to the top, and she could do that? It makes me feel very old!

Alan x

DESCENT

Saturday, July 28, 2018

Photos: Cristian Jarvis

Cristian continues his night-time nature photography rambles, now combined with following Alison during her night-time walks.

The GPS tags place these photos at the far side of the roughly circular nature path from PB into the forest, about 1km north.

The first photo shows Alison bending over, but it's not clear what she's looking at. In the next, Alison is facing a thin, dark figure, slightly shorter than her.

The figure's arms reach out to her in the next image, its hands on either side of her head and their faces almost touching.

In the final picture, this person leads Alison by the hand into the forest. It seems that Cristian didn't attempt to follow them or wait to see if Alison emerged from the forest, and returned to his nature photos.

Camera traps

```
I have used the GPS locations on Cristian's photos
to plot where Alison left the path from Pondok
Bahaya with the mysterious old man. Two clips of
them were captured by a video camera about two
hundred metres north of the path.
   The first is about five minutes after Cristian's
last photo of Alison. The angle is poor, but the
old man walks from behind the camera and into the
distance, leading Alison slowly by the hand. He is
stumbling, and Alison's gait is a slumbering march.
They disappear into the darkness.
   The second clip is just over two hours later,
about 20 minutes before Alison wakes the camp. She
runs towards and past the camera, screaming with a
look of wild panic on her face.
```

Diary: Harriet Kelley, morning

Dammit! Why does being a larger woman of middle age make me the mother to every lost girl out here?

I was glad to help Maya after that asshole Cristian assaulted her in front of everyone. It set off something more than just the shock of the moment — every woman has one or two monsters in her closet. I just didn't plan on being the camp counsellor.

Saturday started like every day in the jungle should do, with a terrified woman screaming her lungs out, bursting into yours truly's boudoir, climbing into Tara's bunk above me and sobbing. It's lucky Tara's sleeping outside in her hammock now!

She was up there faster than an orangutan up a tree with a mouthful of bananas. I could hear her through my earplugs but those beds rock like there's a tornado when someone scrambles up them like that. I woke up in a panic and tried to get out of a bed that's locked down like a mosquito net Fort Knox. I pulled out my earplugs, flipped up my eye-mask, clean forgot where I was and whacked my head into the bunk above. My first thought was there was a beast in the room! I tried to get out of the bunk, wrapped my legs in the netting and fell out trussed up like a hog. God help me if I was in a real fix.

When I'd gotten free I saw Alison and asked her what the fuck was going on. I don't normally use language like that outside of the bedroom, but God-damn it, what does anyone expect at the break of dawn?

Folks started knocking on my door, and next door Maya was hollering that Alison's gone. The sight of my unamused face poking around the door is enough to silence the most dedicated Mormons, so things settled down and I was able to turn my attention to the girl blubbering in my top bunk.

Alison said she'd woken up in the middle of the night, couldn't get back to sleep and decided to go beat the morning rush on the bathrooms. All good until she came out of the washroom and saw "something" in the trees. She says it was a person but I don't think she's enough sense left in her head to tell a man from a monkey in the dark. Rendy said it was likely a monitor lizard. In her scrambled-up state it could have been one of those tiny god-damned deer.

So naturally, when you've seen a ghost in the forest you run to the middle-aged American woman. Not the toughest guy in the camp.

Now, I don't blame Alison for being freaked out by a lizard the size of a doberman hissing in the darkness. I would have screamed and locked myself in the toilet for a while. And the sobbing? I guess she's at the end of her tether with so little sleep. Maya, bless her, brought us tea and coffee while I tried to calm the poor girl down, but I'll admit I'm not at my best before my first mug of morning joe. Time and a hot drink did as much good as my gentle words.

I'll head down to the dock for a bitch with Paul as soon as Alison's napping. That girl had better start sleeping and get her shit together, or she's going home. She's fixing to hurt herself or someone else if she's like this for the whole trip.

I got Maya to dig out Alison's diary so I can leave it by her bed. Maybe she can pour some of her crazy into that. By the look of all those weird plants and freaky varmints on the cover, I'd say it's already fit to burst. Part of me was tempted to look inside, but my better angels won out. If a girl's diary ain't secret, I don't know what is.

And we were all thinking Cristian would be the first one leaving this rodeo.

Diary: Tara Fowler, morning

What is wrong with Alison? I can understand not sleeping out here, but screaming the whole camp awake because she thinks she saw a ghost? FFS she's an adult!!! I'm seriously starting to question her claims about being an 'experienced global adventure traveller'.

She won't come out of Harriet's room, she won't even come out of the top bunk. I don't think I could even get her into a boat if we were ready to leave. We have to go downriver in a couple of days to get more fresh water and food, so it doesn't matter if we go a day or two early. I'm just glad Harriet's dealing with it for now.

And now Rendy!! This is supposed to be my safe place. Away from all the stress at home. I wasn't going to talk about all that rubbish for three weeks, but Rendy said he was worried about me and we've got on so well again that I thought "Hey, why not?" and told him a bit about what's been going on with Jason. It felt good to unload.

Rendy looked really angry and said he'd never let anyone do anything like that to me. I know he didn't plan it but it was pretty obvious what he meant. I needed a friend and he's just made it about him. And I was so gobsmacked I totally friend-zoned him. Bloody men. Even the good ones are idiots! He's been very polite to me all day, but we usually have a chat after lunch to see how things are going, and we need to discuss Alison. I don't want it to be difficult now.

At least it's Saturday. Everyone except Alison is working hard again, and hopefully they'll forget about this madness. They're putting foundation posts for the new kitchen at one end of the hall, and new floorboards at the other. We'll take the group for a walk this afternoon and plant some more trees where the fire killed the forest last year. It should give us all a chance to relax.

I wish I had someone else to talk to here. Maya's still pissed at me over the Cristian thing, I barely know Dewi and Harriet looks like she's had her fill of mothering people. I thought this coordinator thing would be more fun than being the boss at home.

Diary: Dewi Rifqi, midday

Poor Alison. She has been in Harriet's room all day. The old lady even had to take her dinner in tonight, and I do not think she is very pleased to have a mad woman in the top bunk. I think we will have to send her home when Rendy and Tara go down the river.
Bimo and Revo were not sympathetic. They are sure that she saw an animal, perhaps a deer reaching up to eat the leaves on a tree, but they started laughing as they went to look around the toilet block. Rendy should have told them to keep it quiet, but I think he might have even laughed with them.

Ibu Intan is no better. When Bimo and Revo told her what had happened, she nodded and said: "It is the sundel bolong." The sundel bolong is the spirit of a pregnant unmarried woman who was buried alive in an unmarked grave as a punishment in the old days. She gives birth in the grave and the child has clawed its way out of her back. Now she wants to claim the souls of men who wrong women. It is a story my grandmother used to tell us to make sure we were good girls and boys. "Perhaps it is here for Cristian," says Ibu Intan. Stupid woman. Although if it was true, I doubt that anyone would stop it.

Then Revo has his say. "No, it's a pocong." Now that was just what my grandfather would have said. A pocong is a person who has been buried and the ropes around the shroud have not been cut to release his soul, because they have been killed and placed in an unmarked grave. It wants someone to cut the ropes, but an evil pocong can exchange his soul for your soul if you get too close. But a pocong can only hop because of the shroud, and grandfather would chase us around, hopping with his feet together. We would always all scream and laugh and run away from him until he caught one of us and tickled them half to death. I was always too smart to get caught. "Dewina," he said. "You are too clever. No man will ever catch up with you." I thought it was a compliment but when I got older I did not think he was being kind.

I laughed and Bimo turned to me with those little piggy eyes and said: "Oh, Dewi, do you think you are too clever to believe in spirits? You should listen to Ibu Intan, she has many grandchildren and knows the world. How many grandchildren will you have?"

He is a harsh man!

"No, Dewi is right," said Rendy. I was so relieved. "Bimo, that was rude. Ibu Intan, do not go filling their heads with silly old folk tales. It was just an animal." Ibu Intan made a sort of grunting noise that acknowledged him and disagreed at the same time, and Rendy asked me to talk to him in the office.

I thought he was worried about the project or about Alison, but instead he said he had declared his love to Tara and that she had rejected him. He asked me what he should do. What should he do? Stop trying to win the attention of an older woman from the other side of the world who just comes here to escape her problems. Find a suitable young Indonesian woman who wants to live here in the rainforest with him. This is a woman who I know very well.

That is what I did not say, because I do not want to be rejected. I told him that he was very lucky because even if Tara wants him, the Founder would have to fire him because those are the rules.

I will spend the rest of my afternoon checking the camera traps when I have finished this. I have no-one here to talk to except my diary. Perhaps I will see a ghost and I can talk to it. Or an orang. I would get more sense from either of those. And none of them will tell Rendy if they see my tears.

Letter: Alison Pierce to Manny James

Manny4me,

Sorry honey. No sexy talk today. Something weird happened to me last night. Everyone thinks I'm a crazy fool. Made up some bullshit for them. Here's the truth.

Went out again last night. Wandered along the path again. Felt so good again. Don't know how long I was out there. Saw a man on the ground. Almost stepped on him. Mostly naked. Looked old and sick. Must be local but not like the Indonesians in the camp. Touched him. Don't know why. Had to do it.

Grabbed my hand.

Eyes opened.

Looked at me and[8]—

Don't know what happened next. Really don't know. Running back into the camp. Almost dawn. Screaming. Woke myself up. So

---

[8] There is a gap here where Alison has written something for a few lines and then scribbled over until it's illegible.

loud. Ran into Harriet's room. Don't know why. Jumped into top bunk.

Told everyone I saw someone by the toilets. All think I'm crazy now. All want the crazy person to go home. Like when I told my last bloke about the voices. When I told anyone but you.

The voices, though. Not gone but under something else. Like in the jungle. It's so gentle. I could go to sleep.

It's OK. I'll come home to you. Stay here in this bed with Fat Old Harriet under me. Sleep here. Sleep in a nice big warm bed in a quiet hotel room. No noise, no walking through the fucking jungle to have a wee, no animals, no bugs. No bites. I've got so many bites. And sleep. I want to sleep. Can sleep now.

Miss you babe. Ali xx

Email: Imogen Nicholson to Alan Caudwell

To: alan@caudwell.org.uk
From: founder@saveorangutans.org.uk
Subject: Re: Pondok Bahaya diaries - July 28
Date: 30 August 2018 21:13

Alan,

I am so sorry I wasn't able to visit you today. It has been non-stop from before the sun came up, meeting Pak Rafi, our staff families and the police. The families want to know what has happened to their loved ones, and after two weeks they also want to know if they will still be paid while they are missing. We all have bills to pay, I suppose. At least I could reassure them that I hadn't thought of cutting them off. I wouldn't even dream of it!

The police will not tell me anything about what they have found at PB. Pak Rafi thinks this means that they have not found anything, because they would have to tell the families if they were sure that anyone was dead. I hope he is correct, but I cannot help thinking that they have not announced a search of the surrounding area. They will only say that the investigation is ongoing.

I've just seen The Sun's interview with Alison's boyfriend, Emmanuel. For all that they try to paint him as a classic 'love rat', it sounds like they're just old-fashioned swingers in the age of the internet. I think he wanted to explain what happened to her after she was concussed in that cycling accident and started sleeping with different people to drown out the noise in her head. He seems to love her all the same. I can't imagine why she thought that being in the jungle would help.

Unfortunately she's now "Crazy Jungle Nympho Alison" who was planning "steamy rainforest romps". Our PR is earning every penny I can't afford to pay her, but she's asking me questions I can't answer. Of course we have rules of conduct and we interview the volunteers in advance, but they're not children. Relationships happen and we just have to hope they'll be careful and discreet. You can't plan for someone like this, let alone for two of them!

I'm exhausted, upset and frustrated in equal measure. I'd like nothing more than to sit down with an old friend tonight. I would love to see you, but you should continue to keep a low profile.

Jenny x

Sunday, July 29, 2018

Photos: Cristian Jarvis

Cristian obviously wasn't worried about dangerous animals stalking the forest when he set out on another night-time photography expedition. The time-stamps on his photos indicate that he left the camp later than usual, at around 4am, and encountered Alison as he left the camp.

The image is another noisy night-time picture. There are a few trees in the foreground and the lack of structures places it outside the main collection of camp buildings, although the GPS tag is so close that it is hard to be sure.

Based on maps and my recollection of Pondok Bahaya, the photo covers an area north-east of the main camp, where the nature path leads towards the bird-watching tower. The area is about the size of a five-a-side football pitch, where the forest was cut back and used for a variety of purposes from storage to tree-planting. It appears that the photographer is trying to stay out of sight at one side of the clearing, beside the accommodation

```
building for the volunteers. The hammock used by
Tara Fowler would have been to the left of the
photographer, near to the same side of the
clearing.

   In the distance is a white-skinned figure in grey
leggings and long-sleeved top, with long dark hair,
walking out of the forest on the far side of the
clearing. It is impossible to make out a face, but
of all the volunteers and staff, the most likely
subject is Alison Pierce.

   Cristian wouldn't have been able to reach the
path to the birdwatching tower without going
directly past Alison. If he took any photos of the
events which soon followed, they must have been
deleted later.
```

Diary: Maya Pollard, morning

This isn't fun any more. I thought everything had calmed down after Alison's crazy yesterday. I planted a couple of trees and Cris was almost like a normal level of idiot. I've had like, adult conversations with Paul and Harriet for two nights in a row. They're cool people for olds.

And now what? Someone attacked Tara in her hammock and she's hurt, like badly hurt, and I don't think I'm the only girl who was thinking of getting her freak on with someone here.

OK Maya, rewind and get it all down.

Tara was attacked last night while she was sleeping in her hammock. And if you think Alison has a loud scream, that's nothing compared to Tara rolling around on the ground in her hammock, crying and fighting to get out. Whatever happened, it wasn't an animal or a ghost. Someone kicked the shit out of her. We all heard her screaming and crying but there was no-one there when we got out of our rooms, and she was just rolling around on the floor trying to get her mozzie net open so she could get out of it. I mean, fuck, she's got like a black eye and her mouth was bleeding and there was blood in her hair and she was holding her arm like it was broken or something and she's probably got loads of other bruises under her clothes. She looks like shit. And suddenly we're all like, are there locks on these doors? Are they any good? Who am I sharing with?

So Tara had put her hammock up between a couple of trees up behind the building us volunteers sleep in, far enough away that Harriet's snoring would just blend into the jungle noise. Rendy and Rangga are sleeping in the office while we're here, so by the time me and Harriet and Paul and Cris got there, just behind Bimo and Revo, they were already helping her out, but when she saw Rendy she just burst into tears and reached for him, and he tried to hug her like super-gentles but she was just screaming about how everything hurt. Well, yeah, the tears are totally acceptable but that was not the kind of "save me" hug you give to someone you don't already like.

The only person who didn't come out was Alison, who's having a full freak of her own in Harriet's room all of a sudden, just screaming. Rendy turns round and shouts to Dewi to get the satellite phone and first aid kit from his office, and tells the local boys to get Tara something to sit on. Harriet looks like she wants to help but I can tell she can hear Alison screaming and she doesn't want that job again and then of all the people, Cris is just like "I'll talk to Alison" and he's gone.

Me and Paul and Ol' Harry are just standing there like a bunch of lemons, looking at each other and looking at the four of them in front of us, and looking around at the forest and wondering what the fuck did this. Tell you what, I thought, I'll settle for someone blaming an angry orangutan right now cos there's no-one else here and that means one of us did this.

I was just about to suggest we made a cup of tea when Dewi runs back with the first aid box and no sat-phone. It's gone, she says. Rendy looks angry for a second, like she's stupid, but then he's like "are you sure?" and she's like "I checked it on Monday". He's like "I checked it on Friday and it was in the usual place. We'll have to look for it when the sun comes up." He takes the first aid box and lifts Tara up to get a good look at her. He takes his top off, just like that, and starts to dab gently at her face with his shirt but she's wincing every time he touches her.

Rangga gets up and takes a look at the mess Tara's hammock's in. He holds up the string, makes this low, slow, whistle, and says something to Rendy. Then he looks at me and makes a hand motion like someone cutting the cord with a knife. Well it's not like there's a shortage of knives here and the men all have those crazy sharp Indonesian jungle knives. Rangga's always got one. We've got a bit of a friendship going on since he stepped in for me with Cris the other night, just chats after dinner about his life and stuff, and asking each other the words for things. And he smokes, so I can have one too. I felt like I should make the effort to get to know the Indonesians after coming all the way here, and he's interested so it's better than just talking about home stuff with the others. I mean, I've never met anyone who didn't grow up in a place that's much different to where I came from. Everyone at uni's kind of the same, you know? It doesn't hurt that he's got a nice body and kind of a pretty face for an older guy. And I mean older. I think he's at least 40 but he doesn't look like any 40-year-olds I know. I know 30-year-olds who look older than he does.

Anyway, it's all a bit too real for me, so I tell P + H my tea plan and they're on it. Turns out Ibu Intan's already ahead of us, boiling the water and putting out the cups, but I think she's glad of the help and the company. She looks as scared as the rest of us TBH. We take tea and coffee over to Tara and the others, Paul takes some to Cris and Alison. It sounds like somehow he's talked her out of screaming anyway. Who knew he had people skills?

Tara hugs the cup with her good hand and tries to explain what happened but she doesn't know, not really. She starts crying as soon as she tries to put it all together. One minute she was asleep the next minute her head hit the ground and she got a foot in the face. Again and again. She thinks she didn't start screaming until he — I'm saying he — started kicking her in the ribs and belly. Eventually they get her to stand up between Rendy and Rangga, and they walk her to Dewi's room, Harriet takes Dewi in with her and they shut the door to have a better look at her. No-one here's a real doctor or even a nurse.

This is serious shit. Who would do something like that? I mean she was a bit of a bitch to me but I can't imagine what would make me hurt someone like this. I'm pretty sure I could rule out Harriet and Paul. Can't imagine little old Ibu Intan or smiley Revo doing anything like that. Dewi's so gentle she wouldn't hurt a fly. Rendy looked like he'd been punched when he saw Tara. I'm pretty sure he'd kill the person who hurt her. Bimo's got a temper, but he's almost as angry as Rendy about this. I'm not sure Alison knows what day it is. So that leaves Cris. He's sketchy AF but I don't know. I don't want to think about how close I got to him.

It's like 7am now and my brain's burned out. Rendy said we should all go to bed if we can and we'll have the morning off. I'll see how it goes.

Diary: Tara Fowler, morning

Harriet said I should write down what happened. I don't know what good it will do. I don't know any more than anyone else except my body hurts all over and I feel dizzy. I've done a bit of boxing but nothing has ever hurt like this. I'm lying in Ibu Intan's bed, covered in bruises with one eye half closed and a head full of paracetamol, writing very slowly.

One minute I was asleep and the next minute someone was kicking me in my face and head. I think they would have killed me if they hadn't started kicking me in other places too. I couldn't stop them. I was just trapped in the dark, all wrapped up in the hammock and mosquito net until Rendy and Rangga got me out of it.

That's all I know.

My left arm hurts like hell and my ribs hurt like hell and my head is just sore and I want to wash my hair to get all the blood out. Harriet wiped my face a bit but it hurts everywhere. Rendy says the hammock and pillow and stuff stopped me getting cuts instead of these bruises. I guess that's something but Jesus it hurts. One of my teeth is wobbly and my nose is just throbbing. I'm pretty sure it's broken but Rendy says it's just sore. It hurts to breathe and he's worried I've got a broken rib, but I need a doctor to look at that.

The mad thing is that this is exactly what that bastard Jason said he'd do to me, but he's thousands of miles away. No. I'm not going to think about him.

I want to go to sleep but Rendy said he wants me to stay awake for at least half the day because of concussion and stuff before he's sure I'm ready to get in the boat tomorrow.

Harriet's going to stay with me and try to keep me awake, but if I try to write any more I think I'll vomit.

Diary: Rendy Dhanu Saradina, midday

I cannot believe that this has happened in my camp. Who could have done such a thing, and to Tara of all people? She loves this place and gives her time to these people with nothing asked in return.

My first concern must be for Tara's health and safety, to get her to medical care as soon as possible, but I must also think about the safety of all of the volunteers and the staff here. I must think clearly and try not to let my feelings for Tara put other people in danger.

The nearest doctor is more than two hours away by boat and my worst fear is that the damage to her head is more than the black eye and broken teeth and bruising that I can see. She does not know how many times she was kicked in the head, but I think that the attacker did not expect her to be able to call for help when he began to kick her in other places. Harriet and Dewi tell me that she is bruised heavily down to her hips, which appears to be the moment when she began to scream. She may have broken ribs and other internal injuries.

Under normal circumstances I would call for a doctor to attend to her, and for police to investigate, but we cannot find the satellite phone. Dewi and I have both examined the office where it is kept, and it is nowhere to be found. I have heard of monkeys stealing phones when they have been placed in sight, but I have not heard of them taking them out of drawers or out of buildings which are normally shut. We do not lock our doors out here in the rainforest, so any person could have taken the phone when the office was not occupied.

My choices are to fetch a doctor today, if the doctor is available in Camp Pail, or to wait until tomorrow in the hope that Tara is sufficiently recovered to travel to Camp Pail and continue down the river to Pangkalanbun. I am sure that she is too badly hurt to travel today. I will also need to contact the police and the Founder.

Will they come here and interview everyone, or will they ask me to take them back to PKB? For their own safety, I would prefer to take everyone down the river, but we cannot do so in a day with two small boats. It usually takes a couple of days to hire a boat, and I do not want to leave for very long.

I have no doubt that there is someone or something dangerous here in the camp or close by. This attack was planned for the time after Rangga, Bimo and Revo had gone to bed, and before Ibu Intan rose to begin preparing breakfast for the day. I think the attacker used a parang to cut the rope nearest to Tara's head. All of the Indonesians here have a parang, myself included. The kitchen also includes several very sharp knives.

None of my team is capable of such an attack, and the parangs are often left on the work site. As for the volunteers, only Cristian and Maya could have any motive to attack Tara. They were both angry with her earlier in the week, but Tara and Maya have been friendly since Cristian's unfortunate behaviour — Tara asked me not to call it an attack. Cristian is the strongest suspect, but even so I cannot see it in him. I want to believe in the best in people.

Ibu Intan has again been talking to Bimo and Revo about evil spirits. I must ask her not to do this. They are both on edge and too willing to believe in sundel bolongs and pocongs. Evil spirits might do many things, but they do not cut ropes and try to kick people to death.

My immediate concern is to take Tara to a doctor and remove Alison from the camp. She is too unstable to stay here. After that I am not sure what to do.

Alison's problems were not serious enough to bring an end to the project, but this is different. It breaks my heart to think that Pondok Bahaya will be in a worse state than it was when this project began. The meeting room is barely a wooden frame and the kitchen is nothing but a lean-to tent. This place is like a part of me, and I cannot help feeling that I have failed.

Letter: Alison Pierce to Manny James

```
The drawings in Alison's diary begin to change here.
The foliage thickens and looms over the cute animals,
and starts to reach across the text, with pairs of
eyes hidden in the leaves and branches.
```

Manny it's wonderful.

My voices are still gone. A new voice spoke to me. She showed me the jungle's beauty. We walked so far. Don't know where. Barefoot. Just my pyjamas. No bites. Can't be touched now.

Had a nightmare. Woke screaming. Don't remember coming back. Cris found me. Came to my bed. His hand caressed my cheek. I looked into those deep blue eyes. I felt safe again. He helped me out of bed. Strong hands on my hips down the funny ladder with its stupid steps. Yes, I felt very safe. Sat with me on Harriet's bed. Listened to me.

Told him about the thing I saw before. The thing I made up. Not the old man. People should believe me he said. He heard strange noises in the forest at night too. Felt wrong to lie to him. It's my story now. For everyone but you. He's not you babe. No matter what.

Nosey Paul brought us tea and coffee. Cris showed him out so cleverly. We could be together alone. Asked me about home and work. Asked — haha — if I have a boyfriend. Sorry Manny said I don't have a boyfriend when I'm travelling. You know that old line. Always gets me where I want to be.

Cris liked that. Put my hand on his thigh. Felt the muscles in those short shorts he sleeps in. He didn't move away. Put his arm around me. Talked together til Harriet came in. Fat old bird said we should all get some rest. I said I could go back to my room with Cristian's help. SHE ROLLED HER EYES!!!

Outside Cristian put his arm around me. Said he'll look after me. Looked at me with those beautiful blue eyes. I felt beautiful. Wanted him in my room but Maya might come. Gave him a little kiss on the lips. He touched my breast through my pyjamas. I shivered. Want him so much [...]

Maya surprised to see me when she came in. Didn't tell her about Cristian. She had her chance. Says Tara was attacked last night. Bruises all over her face and body. Can't let her sleep yet in case she has concussion or a head injury. Who could do that?

Who or what?

I heard it, I heard it. Heard her head crack on the ground. Heard feet thump into her soft body. Heard the screams that drove it away. My screams. My nightmare. Can't tell. It wasn't me. I wasn't there.

So confused babe. Wish Cris was you. […]

Ali xx

Email: Alan Caudwell to Imogen Nicholson

To: founder@saveorangutans.org.uk
From: alan@caudwell.org.uk
Subject: Pondok Bahaya diaries - July 29
Date: 31 August 2018 16:36

Jenny,

Whatever happened out there, it looks like this is where it started. Something was wrong with Alison, but how could one woman make everyone disappear? We know they were about to bring her and Tara home, and they never made it. I should have some answers for you in a few days. I'm going to plough on and get through it as fast as possible.

Alison's parents were on This Morning, I see. They obviously don't like Manny, but I wonder if he understood her problems better than they did? I think they just thought the doctors could give her some pills and make everything go away.

Don't despair: the media will burn out soon if this is all they've got. There might be a few more kiss-and-tell stories from Alison and Cristian's ex's but I don't think there will be any more surprises. It looks like your PR is doing her best to promote all of the amazing things your volunteers have achieved, and that will come out on top.

I wish I could give you something positive to tell the families. It will be a relief when there is a break in the storm and we can have that dinner. I'm getting a touch of cabin fever stuck in here with all this madness unfolding in front of me.

Alan x

Monday, July 30, 2018

Diary: Paul Dickerson, early morning

Alison must go. I do feel sorry for her, but she must go with Tara today. Or even just go with Rendy to get a doctor. They can send her home from there. It's bad enough that the sky came falling down last night after everything else that has happened, but to wake up in a rainstorm and see her standing in the mud in her grey pyjamas, soaking wet and screaming at the trees with lightning flashing across her face and thunder just booming overhead, it's enough for the rest of us to begin going insane.

Once again, I must give unexpected credit to Cristian. For all of his vanity muscles and ugly man-jewellery, he was the one who picked up a towel, ran half-dressed into the deluge and put it around her shoulders. I don't know what he said to her, but he put his arm around her and walked her into her room. Harriet looked relieved that she had dodged that bullet this time, but she's obviously suspicious of Cristian.

There's nowhere to stand around and chat now—the rain is so heavy it splashes back under the roof over the veranda outside our rooms, so with the drama over I was about to go back inside when Maya came out of the room she shares with Alison. "It's too much guys, too much. Can I have that top bunk?" she asked Harriet, who said she was very welcome. Lovely lady.

Maya took her sleeping bag and now Cristian has been alone in there with Alison for most of the night. I can hear them talking but not what they say because of the rain and thunder. Her voice is quite urgent and his is very calm and soothing. I want to get some rest before dawn, so I will update this when I awake.

* * *

Still nothing from next door, but it is quiet so I suppose I should be grateful for small mercies.

At any rate, it looks like we may have more important problems than Cristian taking advantage of a deranged woman. The rainstorm was too heavy for the tent covering the kitchen, and there were several very bad leaks last night. One of the water dispensers fell over and split apart, but everyone thought it was just another thunderclap.

Rendy and Dewi said they will now try to get us all back to Pangkalanbun. It would be a shame to abandon the project but the attack on Tara has scared us all. I do not see how we can go on if we do not have enough supplies as well as being in danger.

Diary: Maya Pollard, evening

I'm done with Alison. Seriously, I'm glad she's going back. She needs help.

I didn't even notice the rain last night, and with my earplugs in I didn't hear her get up until she was outside screaming that the jungle wants us to go home. I mean, WTAF?

I'd have gone to Harry's room even if creepy Cris wasn't in Alison's bed all the time now. I can't believe I was into him. Old Harry snores a bit but that is the worst thing you can say about her. Cris though, opportunist much? I know it's great that he got crazy Alison to calm down, but I don't think he's in it for humanitarian reasons. I could tell he was working up to "let's get you out of those wet clothes" and she was not going to say no. Good luck to him, she's 100% bunny boiler material. And whatever they did in there, she got in that boat a lot more chilled out so he did us all a favour.

Anyway, she's gone now, down the river with Rendy and Tara and Revo. Dewi said they'll try to fetch a big boat for us all to pile into. Rendy, now there's a guy who needs something to go the right way. He only wants to get Tara out of here—she had to be practically carried into the boat—and with the sun hardly up he's refereeing a fight between Bimo and Rangga about who's to blame for the kitchen disaster. I thought he was going to either cry or punch one of them before he used some very tasty Indonesian to shut them both up. Rangga told me it was something along the lines of "useless homosexual sons of whores", which is about as harsh as you can get here. He's taught me a lot of words that are NSFW and I've tried to explain some English phrases and swearing. It was dead funny because he didn't understand some of them at all. Like, do they even have horses here?

We've had a real get-to-know-you kind of day after the others went. I was going to help with the kitchen, but Dewi, Paul and Harry were all pitching in with old Ibu Ints. Cris was on the dock I think, or off taking photos. He was gone for most of the day, anyway. I didn't even see him at lunch. Rendy told us all to just take a rest so Bimo was in his room doing fuck knows what — I think he's avoiding Rangga. I thought I'd take a wander up to the bird tower and maybe catch some rays with no-one about, when Rangga asked if he could come with me. We stayed up chatting last night after everyone else went to bed. He's not that chatty when he works — he just flashes that warm smile lots — but it's a different story when we're alone. He wants to know everything about me even when it's hard to understand each other, and he doesn't mind talking about himself, either.

I know he's got a family back home but it doesn't sound like he's super-happy. His first wife died quite young when she was having a baby and he must have loved her from the way he talks about her, and then he got married again because that's what they do here, but he didn't like her very much so he found someone else. So, yeah, he could be a bit of a playa but he's kind of hot and he's nice to be around so maybe he doesn't have to try hard. With Cris it was so obvious he just wanted to have sex and that was fun until he didn't read the signs. I didn't mind the way Rangga looked at me when I took off my shirt to get some sun, but he wasn't trying to jump on me like a dog either.

We didn't do anything, but if we did it's not like I can get sent home anyway — we're going home soon and I probably won't see him again. TBH I just feel safe with him.

I would have spent the whole day with Rangga but Dewi asked us to start tidying up the work site in case we have to leave quickly tomorrow. She can think what she likes — I'll keep talking to him if I want to. And I still got to spend the afternoon with him, just with Paul around while Harriet helped in the kitchen.

It's going to be very quiet tonight. There's just me and Paul on the step now, waiting for dinner. We talked about books, of all things. He's reading some silly old story about three idiots mucking about in a boat on the Thames, but he really loves it, and I tried to describe The Essex Serpent. Mum gave it to me for the trip and it sounded really boring compared to his book. It is TBH. I wonder if he'll swap?

Turns out I've got the same orangutan book as Dewi, by this woman who's been here for 50 years or something. Dewi gets really excited when she talks about orangutans but it's nice to see her smile and maybe now she doesn't think I'm such a slut. She's scared now anyway. We all are.

The vegetables got a good wash last night and there's lots to go around if we're just here for a day or two until the boat comes. Cris came back just now saying he'd got some amazing photos of some bird or other. He's like a different person when there isn't a free woman for him to sniff around. I guess the four of us will chat after dinner but Harry and Paul go to bed early and I don't want to be up on my own with Cris, not even if Dewi is here. I know he seems chill now, but he's still the only person I can think would have attacked Tara.

Maybe I can go for a night walk with Rangga. I could bring him back to my room and I'm sure no-one would notice, but I don't want him to think I'm that easy. I'll stay with Harriet again tonight. There's something reassuring about knowing she's in the bunk underneath me.

Diary: Dewi Rifqi, night

I am very scared. Now I have said it. We are in trouble now and someone is probably dead. Tara is probably dead.

I decided to take the whole group for another night walk after dinner. It was better than just sitting around doing nothing and worrying about what happened to Tara. We got back to the camp and they were back. I knew something was wrong. They were not due back until tomorrow at least. Rendy was frantic with worry. I could hear Alison screaming and crying in one of the rooms, and Revo's bedroom door was shut.

The storm was even worse than we thought. Some big trees were maybe hit by lightning and they have fallen across the river in a place where it is very narrow, but there is also a lot of rubbish washed down from upriver — branches and plants and the like — and it has turned into a dam across the river. They tried to get through but the propeller got caught in the weeds and Revo was trying to fix it while Rendy was trying to push some of the rubbish apart from the front and keep them facing downriver. Alison was trying to help by holding up branches that were coming across the boat. They should have turned around but I know Rendy desperately wanted to get help for Tara.

I do not think anyone is exactly sure what happened, but something brushed against Alison or fell on her neck and she became crazy, rocking the boat and screaming again. Revo tried to grab her, I think, and then Tara woke up to the screaming and the boat lurched and both Tara and Rendy went into the river. Rendy grabbed the boat and hauled himself up, but Tara had gone into all that rubbish. Revo slapped Alison so hard she sat down, but the boat rocked so hard that he fell out also. Rendy had to help him back in but none of them could see Tara. They called many times for her, but the current was very strong and more rubbish was arriving behind the boat. Rendy did not know what to do with Alison if she became dangerous again. He was so angry that he might have thrown her in the river, I think. In the end he had to come back before they got trapped. Even then it was very slow.

I know that I have been jealous of the way that Rendy feels about Tara, but she did not deserve this. She is a good person. If she did not drown, there are crocodiles[9] and false gharials[10] in the river which might eat her if she was weak or unconscious. It is not hopeful.

Now Rendy and I do not know what to do. I mean to say that I do not know what to do and Rendy cannot think. He has been sitting on the dock since he told us what happened to Tara, and I

---

[9] Borneo is home to both the 2m-long critically endangered freshwater Siamese crocodile and the notorious saltwater crocodile, which can grow up to 6m in length.
[10] The false gharial is a large, endangered freshwater reptile, growing up to 5m long. It looks like a crocodile with a long, narrow snout containing 76 to 84 teeth.

do not know what to say to him, but I need him to be in charge. I do not know if the others will even listen to me when I have an idea. Ibu Intan will not stop talking about curses and other superstitious silliness. She claims that Alison is possessed and she is still muttering even after I told her to stop it.

We have no way to contact anyone, and it is not possible to walk through the rainforest to the nearest village. But there is not enough food and water for more than a week, and not enough fuel for the generator unless we are very careful. All of this would normally have been bought with a week to spare. It is possible that our friends and colleagues will come to look for us in a few days if we do not make contact as expected, but in addition there is a dangerous person in the camp and we do not know who it is. I hope that tomorrow I can think of something to do to help us but I do not want to die here. I do not want to die here.

Diary: Harriet Kelley, night

I can't believe that Tara is dead, and that's on Alison. If she was a mad dog they'd have shot her already. Us folks are trapped with her here in the jungle, with no way out and our food and water running out. I've always prided myself on being a strong woman, but this ain't a business rivalry or a dumbass husband fooling around. There's a devil in this camp who was willing to beat young Tara half to death, and whoever it is, we're trapped with them. We're in a poke and I don't like the odds.

I'm sure it was Cristian who beat up Tara last night, but I can't prove it and what good would it do us if I could? We're still stuck with the creepy shit and he seems to be worming his way into Alison's crazy little head. I don't see him fixing to help her get any better. At least Maya got herself free from him. I'm happier having her for a room-mate.

Right now we don't even have a phone. I sure hope Rendy and Dewi can fix us a way to holler for help. Rendy's far from thinking straight tonight, though. It don't take a genius to see he's been holding a torch for Tara and he's too wrapped up in grief to think straight tonight. I'd talk to him but I don't mind saying I'm shit-scared of going outside, now that most everyone else has gone to bed. Maya has taken to sitting out with Rangga. Maybe she shouldn't be fooling with an older man but if it's keeping her mind off the crazy then maybe I'm just sour that I've got no-one to talk to. I wish Paul hadn't gone to bed so early.

Photos: Cristian Jarvis

Taken with a long lens, obviously through dense foliage, this is a photo of Maya and Rangga, sitting on a wooden platform in the sun.

Google Earth shows a dark square at the far side of the looping path which the staff used to take visitors on nature walks through the rainforest. It's about a kilometre north of the main camp, and the OST confirms that there's a large wooden platform here, about five metres across, which is used for everything from picnics and teaching to stargazing.

Other photos suggest that Maya would usually wear a loose shirt around the camp, but here she's wearing only a vest top, rolled up above her belly, and loose trousers, leaning back with her face to the sky and smiling. Rangga is talking to her and smoking casually, but he's obviously admiring her body. She's wearing sunglasses, so it's impossible to see whether she's aware of his gaze.

Tuesday, July 31, 2018

Diary: Paul Dickerson, early morning

It is hard to believe that yesterday began with poor Tara beaten half to death and ended with her being drowned by that unstable woman. That MAD woman who is in the room next door to me and apparently free to go wherever she pleases. Perhaps she didn't intend to knock Tara out of the boat, and I have always tried to be understanding of people who are undergoing mental stress, but for the safety of everyone here, Alison needs to be locked up. Instead, she seems to have spent the whole night being knocked up by Cristian.

    I have been far too generous to that appalling young man. His displays of kindness and sympathy towards Alison were nothing more than a heartless and calculated plan to seduce someone who is obviously deranged. It is beyond comprehension to me that anyone could think about sex in the shadow of such awful tragedy, yet Cristian obviously offered to 'take care' of Alison with one clear goal in mind. I settled into the din of the jungle very easily but now I am the one who has not slept a wink. Alison very willingly allowed Cristian to score his goal, in fact she actively encouraged him to do it more than once.

They are thankfully quiet now. Cristian seems to have cured Alison's insomnia at least, and I shall also attempt to make up on my lost sleep as I do not think anyone will be rising early this morning. I have a bottle of water and a container which I am using as a bedpan so I do not have to make any excursions alone during the hours of darkness.

When everyone is up I will speak to Harriet and Maya about Cristian and Alison, and decide what to say to them about their behaviour last night. It cannot be allowed to continue unchallenged.

Letter: Alison Pierce to Manny James

Manny it's different now.

Not confused any more. Couldn't walk last night. Everyone too scared. Alone in my room. The voice spoke to me. Told me Her name.

Rimadan.

She knows me now. Touches my mind. Speaks without words. She's old, babe. In the trees. In the ground. In the river. A hunter.

She feels my needs. For Cris. For You.

I feel Her needs. This is Her place. Not ours. Wanted us to leave. Now She wants to cleanse us. Feed the soil with blood. The old way. The way of Her people. She closed the river to keep us here.

Tara was the first gift. I gave her to the water. Now she feeds the jungle. Rimadan's pleasure tingles tingles tingles from my core to the tips of my fingers and toes. Stronger than any man or woman I have ever been with. Could barely hide it from Rendy and Revo when they were looking for Tara in the water.

Cris saw Her in me. She saw him. Hunters together. United in me. Doubling my power. We are connected.

He brought me the parang. She knows this blade. It waits under my bed. I hum and buzz and hunger. […]

Would you understand? You're kind. A lover. You hate to hurt people. You live to give pleasure. With you I feel good.

She's not. He's not. Just my pleasure. Her pleasure. His pleasure. In me. Through me.

It's new. Different. I like it. Find another babe. I'm sorry.

Diary: Rendy Dhanu Saradina, early morning

I do not know how this project could get any worse.

I have brought death to a wonderful woman and I do not know how to protect the rest of our volunteers. In addition, I am responsible for a group of people who will soon be running out of food and drinkable water. There is no obvious way to leave Pondok Bahaya or call for help.

I have not slept tonight, but I dared not go further than the steps of the office I share with Rangga. There is still a violent attacker at large. I must find a way to call for assistance so that I can save the good people who remain here. There is no way to pass down the river without several boats and tools to clear the river. Most importantly we would need many more able-bodied men than we have here. Up the river there is nothing except the mining camp, and we do not have a good relationship with those people for the obvious reason that their work is poisoning the land and the river. However, they must have a radio or a satellite phone, and they cannot be so bad that they would refuse to help us. They will also need to open the river to obtain supplies and transport their goods.

I will take Revo and Bimo with me. Neither of them like the miners, but Revo is good at easing difficult situations and I will feel more comfortable with Bimo at my side, despite his temper.

I know that Revo also feels terrible about what happened on the boat yesterday. I must apologise for shouting at him on the journey back. He could not have stopped Alison. The current was very strong and it is likely that Tara was carried under the water very quickly. I do not see how she could have survived. If there was a mistake, it was taking Alison with us. I see now that she has gone completely mad and has no morals or emotions that I can understand. I would leave her alone her if I could, but I know that is not what Tara would want.

I will explain what happened to the authorities and to Tara's family. It is my responsibility and I do not care what punishment I must face. I can face no worse punishment than the knowledge that I put Tara in fatal danger.

I do not expect that I will be able to return to the forest when all of this is over. I do not expect to keep this job and I doubt I will be able to get another like it. My life will be over.

The best that I can do is to ensure that the people in this camp are able to safely return to their families and loved ones, with one exception. Alison must face justice, for I am now sure that it was she who attacked Tara in the beginning. I do not understand why, and I am wary of making any accusations until we have left the forest. She could become even more dangerous.

Diary: Paul Dickerson, morning

It appears that I slept very soundly indeed. It is after 10am and I can see no-one in the camp from my door. I can hear some talking from Cristian and Alison in the next room, and on the other side I can hear nothing, which means that Harriet is not sleeping. I hope that she and Maya were not disturbed by their neighbours as I was.

I have observed that the jungle din and the trees themselves seem to soak up a lot of noise, so I doubt that Rendy or the other Indonesians heard anything from our neighbours.

I hoped to talk to Harriet before I lance the boil of my neighbours' behaviour, but I have awoken with a resolve to take action. There is no better time than the present.

Letter: Alison Pierce to Manny James

Manny. Know I said we were over. You deserve an explanation.

I've gone so far now. Don't want to be forgiven. Rimadan released me from guilt.

Always wanted something more. Another holiday. Better job. More men. I serve Her now. No more wants. Only Her needs. Her rewards. Today She gave me blood.

Wonderful, delicious blood!!

So much energy in me. Never thought one person could give so much power. A weak and pathetic old man. What about the rest? Paul was angry about our noise last night. Came to tell us off. Cris saw he was alone. No one near. Pulled him into the room. No match for my great warrior. Up against the wall. Hand covered his screams.

Rimadan knew what to do. So I knew.

Took the parang. Thrust it into the old man. Again. Again. Each time more power filling me. Pushed with all my weight. Parang went through him. Bone cracked. Stuck in the wood. Tugged it out. Hands slipping. Body limp. Paul fell like an empty sack.

SO much blood. Thick hot river of life pouring out onto me. On my hands. Arms. Breasts. Belly. Legs. Does everyone have this rich nectar inside them?

Had to share the power with Cris while it surged through me. Cris held my fingers to my lips. We sucked them clean. Had to have him again. Rimadan riding us both.

No-one in the camp still. Easy to hide the body in the jungle. Rinsed the floor. In the shower gave in to all of our urges. […]

Had to throw away our clothes. Wood stained with Paul's blood. Make sure that no-one else comes into the room. Maya is in Harriet's room now. Need a plan for the next one. So wonderful. So dangerous. Rimadan hungry for more. Strongest first or weakest first? Move carefully. One by one.

Lots of time while the river is blocked. Fuck. Kill. Wait. Repeat. Indonesian men will be hardest. Then the women. Tara was the only other threat.

Rangga and Maya making lunch now like a proper little couple! Must play the same game. Sunshine on the deck. Cris takes his camera for a walk in the forest. Too hard to be around him now. Can't resist. Can't annoy the others. Patience Rimadan.

Wasn't here to save the rainforest. Here to serve it. She will reward me every time. I will serve Her.

***

```
This is the last entry in Alison's diary. Her
writing is frenetic, almost illegible, and scrawls
wildly around the page. It is hemmed in on every
side by doodles of trees with leering faces and
absurdly aroused men, women and animals copulating
in bizarre, grotesque combinations.
```

Instagram: Cristian Jarvis

```
If his Instagram account is accurate, Cristian liked
his partners to pose for a naked 'trophy' photo, using
smiley-faced stickers to obey Instagram's rules on
nudity. It is surprising how many women were willing
to do this, although after seeing the contents of
Cristian's phone, I can confirm that Instagram got the
mild photos.

He also had a unique talent for creating captions and
hashtags which were simultaneously complimentary and
```

```
demeaning to their subjects. The media wasted no time
tracking down his 'rooted henchwomen'.
Alison was the last to accept her accolade, posing
naked in the bathroom at Pondok Bahaya. It is not a
flattering location, but she appears to be very happy.
This is the final post that Cristian prepared for his
account, although he took more photographs in the
following days.
```

@Pecstourist Greatest #henchwoman ever!!!! This one always wants more #rooted #sluzza #filthy #nymphohench #lust #bloodlust #psychohench

Diary: Maya Pollard, evening

I read somewhere that all men are dangerous. It's probably true, but sometimes you have to choose a man who's going to be dangerous to everyone but you. Right now, I think I've made the right choice and I'm sticking with him. Hi mum and dad, this is Rangga, he saved me from psychos in the jungle. Because there are two psychos and they're called Cris and Alison.

How do I know? So Rendy was just a mess this morning after what happened to Tara, I mean we're all totally freaked out TBH but he just wants to get the rest of us home and it's the only thing keeping him going. It's so obvious he was in love with her and I don't know if she liked him back but that doesn't matter now. His new plan this morning is to go up to the mining camp and see if they can help us to call someone out there. It seems like a good plan. I'm on board.

That leaves the rest of us with time on our hands and everyone agreed it would be nice to have some fresh food so Ibu Intan took Dewi and Harriet into the forest to look for fruit and roots and berries and shit. I mean, we're in THE RAINFOREST so it shouldn't be too hard to find something edible. Rangga said he could probably catch a couple of fish so I said I'd help him put worms on hooks or whatever it is fishing people do. The main thing is I wanted to stick by the strongest man in the camp and no-one can sneak up on you at the end of a big long jetty. He's a nice guy, too. He's got questions but he's funny and chilled and sooooo ripped with real muscles.

We had a nice morning. He got a couple of fish and I got to catch some rays and if we're talking in fish metaphors I can tell you he's totally hooked every time I show the old flat belly and tight top. I mean I know it's a bit pale and he's being cool about it but I think he wants to try the white meat and I am completely happy with him thinking about me like that. I might want to try a bit of the dark. Who am I kidding? I totally do, and if it keeps me from getting stabbed by crazy people then I am putting it out there on a plate with all the garnish I can find. Does that make me a bit of a whore? Even if I like him? I'll worry about that when we get out of here.

So with that in mind I went back to my old room to get some fresh clothes and make-up from my big bag. I'm glad I took my washbag and diary and phone and stuff when I went to Harry's room. I could hear Cris and Alison in the shower from a long way off. There was no mistaking what they were doing and they didn't care who knew, so I had time to get my stuff. The floor was wet, which I thought was a bit weird, and then I saw why — they'd been trying to wash away blood and there was a lot of it.

I found a bead bracelet under the bed. Covered in blood. I think it's Paul's and I haven't seen him all day. I think they killed him. Now they're having a shower together!!! What have they done with the body?

I wanted to scream and throw up and sit down and instead I had to hold it all in and this weird little squeak popped out and I just stood there in my room, my empty room, with this scream in my head and this sticky bracelet in my hand and my heart going crazy in my chest.

I wanted to get out of there but now I had to tiptoe around the puddles to get to my stuff without leaving bloody footprints everywhere. I don't know if Rangga believes me or not, though. I mean, I can hardly believe it, and by the time I'd told him they were on their way back so we couldn't check. Thank fuck Alison's so noisy.

Rangga doesn't speak enough English so I had to stop freaking out and mime it and then I remembered about Google Translate on my phone and he was like "Bangsat meraka!"[11] and I was like "Fucking totally bangsat mate!".

He says we should wait for Rendy and the others to come back tonight so we can face them together. I think he could totally take Cris but if they killed him they must have a knife or even one of those big parangs.

I'm so scared now. Glad I'm sharing with Harriet now but I'd rather have Rangga watching over me. I hope Rendy and Bimo and Revo come back soon.

Diary: Harriet Kelley, night

I sure wish I knew where Paul has gotten to. I've gotten to know him pretty well in the past week and he's not one to wander off into the rainforest on his own. I don't know where else he could be, though. Maybe I should have checked on him this morning, but if he wanted to sleep in I figured that was his choice. We don't have a whole lot to do anyway. I've checked his room now, though, and he's not there.

And I've gotta say that I had a nice time with the girls looking for something to eat. I'm not sure I know what we'll be eating tonight but it's good to know these ladies will keep us fed until help arrives. That Ibu Intan sure knows her way around the trees and plants, and Dewi's a different girl when she puts on her walking boots and takes

---

[11] Roughly, Indonesian for "fucking hell".

the lead. She's got cameras all over the place here to watch for those beautiful clouded leopards and things. She even showed us a few videos on her phone this afternoon.

The two of them don't exactly get on, though. They were arguing about ghosts or spirits or something. Ibu Intan said there's an evil spirit in the camp that's to blame for Tara getting hurt and then killed, and for the storm, and Dewi told her to stop being superstitious because it was scaring people. Well, it was scaring her! I don't go in for any of that mumbo-jumbo. God is for Christmas and Easter, and I'll say my prayers at Thanksgiving like any good American, but Hallowe'en is just for kids and weirdoes. But I'm sure Ibu Intan said something else to Dewi, like she was accusing her of something, and that did not go down well. Dewi said something short and nasty and she did not want to translate it. I was glad to just pick the fruits and dig up the roots they pointed at. Those roots are hard work even after a week of sawing and hammering.

Paul wasn't about when we got back and the others were just lazing about. Well, Rangga was cleaning a couple of fish and Maya was trying to prepare some rice, but she doesn't know one end of kitchen from the other and I'd say she was just trying to stay close to Rangga. She looked pretty relieved to see us. I couldn't see Cristian but I was surprised to see Alison out on the deck, soaking up the sun in a bikini top that she probably shouldn't have been wearing, but we're well past worrying about the little rules now, and she was practically glowing with contentment. She didn't look like a crazy woman who had just tipped someone into the river. But nobody was going to bring that up so we just cooked and ate and left some for dinner. Cristian wandered out of the forest just as we were sitting down, shirt off and his camera bag swinging from one hand, and served himself like he was just back from the beach for a hotel buffet. He said hello to everyone and kept a distance from Alison, but I could see the look that passed between them, like electricity.

And nobody else knew where Paul had gotten to. Maya said she'd been on the dock all morning with Rangga. I believe that much, but there was something she wasn't telling. She looked scared. It was a late lunch and by the time we'd eaten and cleaned up the clouds had come over and it was starting to rain. Dewi says it gets like this in the afternoons when the rains come, but it wasn't any cooler.

I came back to my room to write, Dewi went to her office and Ibu Intan went for her usual afternoon nap. Maya and Rangga went down to the little viewing hut on the dock. Ibu Intan and Dewi didn't look too happy about that but I'd say she's safe with him. She won't get anything she doesn't expect anyway.

Last I saw of Alison she was standing in the rain with Cristian, getting soaked. She was just stood there, swaying, hands in the air like she was listening to music that wasn't there. I think she was talking to herself, but the rain was so loud on the roof. He was behind her, grinding on her arse to his own beat, arms wrapped around her. I don't know how long they were out there but I know what they're doing back in that end room right now. Glad I'm a heavy sleeper. It ain't pretty to hear but if it stops her doing any more crazy then I can live with it.

I don't know if Maya's sleeping. She's buried her head under her sleeping bag with her headphones on. There's something eating at her, but I'd wager she's just sore that she can't stay up late with Rangga in this rain.

Where the hell is Paul?

Diary: Rendy Dhanu Saradina, night

Damn Bimo and his prostitute mother. The miners were not friendly but did he have to pick a fight? Did he have to know that man from when he was a logger? All he had to say was hello and keep his damned mouth shut.

I am sure they would have helped us. The foreman was coming around to the idea when I had told him about Tara and Alison. They don't like us but they don't want any attention for not helping us. It might even look good for them. And we all need the river open again.

But it couldn't be that easy. Nothing is that easy any longer. One of the miners used to know Bimo when he was working for some kind of gangster or businessman. I know the story, it's in the files my predecessor gave me. This guy was bringing in logs from the rainforest and gold and whatever else from the mines, and finding people to go and do the work. Bimo had done some illegal logging when he was young and somehow he'd ended up as a local boss or something like that. I guess he could throw his weight around and he was handing out bribes to make things happen or keep the government out of his business, but word has it he was a very different man back then. He even got engaged to the main guy's niece or cousin or something. It was a family connection and he was going somewhere.

Then he met the Founder and they became friends and Bimo somehow fell in love with the rainforest. I think he was taken to Camp Pail or somewhere like that where he saw orangutans up close. He left everything behind and started working for us in the forest. He started telling people they should not chop down trees in the national parks or set up mines without permission. It made a lot of people very angry and his wife-to-be left him for another rising star. I know he was very sad about it, and very angry. Now he's just Bimo.

And because of that he lost his temper when a miner started saying things about that woman and the man she married. And about how she left Bimo for a real man. These are not mild accusations for a man like Bimo or any Indonesian man. Even Revo was angry for his friend. But for Bimo to respond the way he did was very stupid. You do not say that another man's sister is a prostitute who visited the mining camps. You do not say that all of his colleagues had probably had sex with her. Because that man will probably attack you. That man will cut your friend with a parang when he tries to stop the fight. Then you will chop his arm off with your parang and the foreman will give you one minute to get out of his camp.

We did not talk very much on the journey back. Bimo apologised but we were too busy trying to stop Revo from bleeding to death and looking behind us. I was full of anger. I could not find the right words. I knew that I must explain our failure to Dewi and Ibu Intan and the volunteers.

Now Bimo says the miners will come because their friend will die and they will want revenge. They will not come until tomorrow because they will understand that we cannot escape and afterwards they can make it look like we were never here. Bimo knew the man that he killed. He was related to the woman Bimo was supposed to marry. His family will expect justice to be swift and this will settle an old score for someone very powerful, so the miners will be rewarded.

How can I tell these people that there are men coming here to kill them and they will do terrible things to the women? They are already terrified because of what happened to Tara. They know they are trapped.

There must be a way to negotiate with the miners or to threaten them. If only we had the satphone now. How stupid it was to tell them that we have lost it. Can I pretend that we have found it?

Email: Imogen Nicholson to Alan Caudwell

To: alan@caudwell.org.uk
From: founder@saveorangutans.org.uk
Subject: Re: Pondok Bahaya diaries - July 30-31
Date: 1 September 2018 11:41

Alan,

I should thank you for working so hard to get me two days of diaries.

I only wish they weren't so full of tragedy. We're still far from knowing what happened to everyone at Pondok Bahaya.

I finished reading them for the second time an hour ago, then I read it all again, and then I did nothing because I knew that once I write to you, I will have to call Tara's parents. It's bad enough that they have to put up with that nasty ex of hers pretending he's concerned about her. I'm sure he only wants to be in the spotlight. They don't deserve this.

I can tell you a little more about what my staff found when they broke through to Pondok Bahaya. The wooden buildings had been burned down — the hall and the accommodation block. To be honest, they said the hall looked like it had been blown up and then burned down. The brick buildings — the staff bedrooms, the office and the toilets — they were still standing but badly scorched. One of the two staff bedrooms was covered in dried blood and only the bed frames remained, the other had one bloody mattress and one clean, but it hadn't been used for days. The office had been ransacked.

I think the police are conducting a criminal investigation into what they found. I will have to tell them what happened to Tara and Revo, and about the dispute with the miners. I'll send someone over tomorrow to pick up the diaries and everything else — you have copies, so you can carry on putting the story together. Who knows, the police might even pay you to help them?

If they don't arrest me tomorrow, I'll break you out of that hotel room for dinner at that little place outside of town.

And don't forget to get enough rest. I can't have you going mad as well!

Jenny x

Wednesday, August 1, 2018

Diary: Rendy Dhanu Saradina, early morning

I have a few moments to leave what may be the final entry in my journal. Everyone here understands what may happen today. Perhaps they do not understand, but they agreed that we should show our strength and then attempt to negotiate. I do not know what The Founder would do if she were here, but I hope that she would approve. After all that has happened I do not expect to keep my position here if I survive this day, but I have done everything in my power to keep these people safe.

I told the women to leave the camp and attempt to escape through the forest, but they have refused. Two of them have even volunteered to fight alongside the men, and everyone has worked through the night to build our defences. I was surprised that Rangga was so creative.

There are four men here to defend five women — I would not count Paul if he was even here, and that is another problem I do not have time to think about.

I have not been in a fight since I was a youth, and never anything like this, but I will not let them destroy my camp. I must defend them all, even Alison and that young fool Cristian. I am told that British and American women want to be equal to men. They will need to be as strong as the men if we are to have a chance of survival. Even so, I have told them to run to the forest if we are losing the battle.

Cristian looks strong but I cannot tell if it is all swagger to impress Alison. I know that Bimo will fight like a demon. Rangga has a quiet resolve that I know I can rely on. Maya is terrified but she is determined to be useful. She has more strength than I at first thought. I do not know what to think of Alison. She may be as dangerous to us as she is to the miners.

We can expect at least 10 miners and they will be armed better than we are. We have a few parangs, an axe, a chainsaw and some tools. They will have all of the same and perhaps some shotguns. They may even have explosives from the mine.

They will come as soon as it is light, but they must come up the jetty to enter the camp, and we will surprise them there. If they will not negotiate, then Allah will decide if we deserve to live. For those in my care, I pray that he is merciful.

Diary: Dewi Rifqi, evening

I wonder if any of us will live to tell the tale of what happened here at Pondok Bahaya?

We thought that the miners had not waited when Rendy began banging on our doors late last night. We must prepare, he said, and he confided to me that if Tara's attacker is still among us then it would be best to keep everyone busy all night. And so he told us his plan. Rangga and Bimo had some thoughts of their own, and Alison said that the forest would protect us. She sounds like the indigenous people I read about at uni.

The miners arrived with the dawn as we expected, floating silently down the river in two low boats. They tied them up and crept out, but the monkeys which sleep in the trees opposite the jetty did not enjoy being disturbed. Perhaps Alison was right. The forest is on our side.

Rendy came from behind a tree at the head of the dock as the miners gathered at the far end. He called out to the leader and told him to go back. He said he would not allow them to enter Pondok Bahaya. He promised that more miners would die.

The leader spoke to his men and told Rendy that they would kill all of the men and take any women back with them. He said they would care for the women until help arrived from down the river. We were all listening from the trees, beyond where the miners could see. I did not believe this promise.

Rendy said it was not acceptable. He told the miners to return to their camp and forget about us.

Their leader said he could not forget that one of his people had died slowly overnight. He demanded justice.

Rendy told him to wait for the authorities to arrive.

This was not the kind of justice that he wanted, the leader replied. The miners began to walk up the dock.

Rendy slipped back into the trees and returned to us, shaking his head. He apologised to us, and we moved to our positions.

Rendy's plan was simple, but as brilliant as anything I would expect from that man. We allowed the miners to come up the dock until they came across our barricade. We had placed it at the top of the steep path from the dock, just before it grows wider and invisible to the miners until they had begun to climb towards it. It stretched into the trees, several metres beyond the path so that the miners would not be tempted to walk around it and seek the path Rendy had taken. It is fortunate that we have so much junk from the old main hall. They had to climb across the barricade, and were unable to see well into the camp until they were on top of it. When they did so, the camp would appear empty.

Maya was concealed in the forest at the far end of the barricade with a lighter. The men had all wanted her to stay with Ibu Intan, Harriet and myself in Revo's room at the top of the camp, but she made it clear that we needed someone to light the barricade. She and Rangga shared a look and he said he agreed with her. Reluctantly, perhaps. Rendy did not seem happy but he said he did not have time to argue. Cristian did not object to her risk, either. I do not know if this is because he hoped she would die or because he was standing up for equal rights. Perhaps I should have volunteered, but I do not think that I would be of any use and Revo needs my care.

It was only as they crossed the barricade that the miners smelled the petrol and saw the sheets stuffed between the planks. Their leader was among them, and he did not pause.

Four of the miners had cleared the barricade before Maya lit it, but two of them were halfway across and another had started to climb it. The flames flew through the sheets and the wood, and those three men were inside a wall of fire before they could get away.

I will never forget the sound a man makes when his clothes catch fire around him, let alone three men. It is a howl of pure torment that I do not ever wish to hear again. I am sure the whole jungle went silent as those screams echoed into the trees. I knew in the moment that what we had done was wrong, but I also knew that we had no other choice. These men would not care for us in any way that we would recognise.

Two of those at the front tried to drag their colleagues free and their leader — armed with a shotgun, kept watch and tried to see who had started the fire.

Rendy appeared as the leader was isolated and the men on the dock were trying to get the third man out of the wall of flames.

Rendy had a crude spear — just a blade attached to a thin ironwood pole, but I thought that he looked magnificent as he stepped out from behind the old hall. The leader looked surprised by the weapon, and he was obviously concerned that someone was still in the forest. Rendy told him we would let the survivors go if they put down their weapons and left us now. He promised to care for the wounded men.

The leader seemed to be considering Rendy's offer, but one of the men on the dock shouted something about revenge. He raised his shotgun. I could not hear what he said because of the roar from a chainsaw starting up on the hill at the far end of the barricade from Maya.

Cristian ran down from the forest on the right, screaming and swinging the chainsaw in the air. It is almost comical how much the sound of a chainsaw growling into life can place fear into the hearts of men who want to kill you. I am not sure if Cristian was entirely in control of it, but it froze the miners in their boots, even as their burning colleagues screamed for help.

Rangga came out of the forest nearby with a hoe in his hand and hurled it at one of the men facing to the barricade. He had sharpened the wide blade for hours overnight, but no-one was certain if it would be an effective weapon. It hit the man on his left hip and he cried out, but when it slid away I thought he was not badly hurt. Slowly the blood began to spread across his shorts and his leg turned red. He tried to turn and run away, but after two or three steps towards the forest, his left leg folded beneath him as if it was made of paper. Rangga drew his parang and stepped forward to finish him, a grim look on his face.

Cristian descended on the last miner, whirling his chainsaw as the man cringed before him. Behind the barricade, the plan was for Bimo to slip off the sacks under which he had been hiding, then attack those trapped below the fire while they were confused and trying to save their fellows.

The leader was by now very distracted, so Rendy threw his spear. He's not a fighter and it went past the leader's head. The leader shot at him in a wild panic, but the shotgun's broad blast showered Rendy's right arm and chest with shot. My dear Rendy fell down.

The last miner who had come over the barricade was edging around downhill into the forest looking for Maya when Alison screamed out of the trees with a parang. She was supposed to wait for an opportunity to take someone by surprise, but no-one expected her to be naked and covered in mud. The miner was far too distracted to raise his own blade, and by the time his arm went up she'd smashed her parang into his shoulder and knocked him over. She is a skinny woman and he was a sturdy-looking man. I think he fell over in shock at the savagery of her attack.

Alison went over on top of him, but rolled off while he was clutching his shoulder. She had dropped her parang so she started kicking him — she still had her boots on! — and then she picked up the miner's parang and started hacking at him with it. The look of glee on Alison's face and her squeals of joy made me shiver. She wasn't just trying to kill him, she was enjoying it.

I couldn't see what was happening on the dock, but Maya told me she saw it all from the forest. Bimo ran at the miners' backs as they tried to pull one of their colleagues off the burning barricade. He killed one of the miners before they saw him, and when they turned he killed another and wounded two more very badly before the last one recovered from the surprise and struck a terrible wound. Bimo fell and she saw their blades rise and fall until they left him for dead.

On the uphill side of the barricade, the leader left the other miners to fight Cristian and Rangga. He prowled forward over Rendy's body with his shotgun moving warily ahead of him. He must have still had a shell in the second barrel, and he was about to shoot Rendy again when Alison appeared from the forest and attacked the miner on his right.

When his attention returned to Rendy, he must have seen that he was no threat but he also saw me before I could close the door to Revo's room. Our eyes locked across the camp and I knew he would come for us. Maybe he thought he could take us hostage. I closed the door, hoping its flimsy lock would hold him off, and shrank back as far as I could into the far corner of the small room. Harriet swore that no-one would hurt me and stood in front of me with one of Ibu Intan's sharp cleavers, but Ibu Intan was possessed of an even more powerful matriarchal impulse and crouched before the door, gripping a long, thin knife used for gutting fish.

The leader rattled the door and Ibu Intan screamed at him to stay away. Seconds later he burst through, into the wild face of Ibu Intan and her knife. He looked shocked and said nothing as the blade sank between his ribs. I do not know if she knew where to stab him or if she was simply lucky. It seemed like instinct that made him push her back with the knife buried in his chest. I am ashamed to say that I screamed like a small child as Harriet stepped forward, cursing colourfully in English, and chopped the cleaver into his shoulder. This time he screamed and I closed my eyes as scarlet blood squirted from his shoulder onto the ceiling above.

I heard Ibu Intan curse in a Dayak dialect that I do not know. When I opened my eyes Ibu Intan had pulled her knife from his chest, where the blood spread thickly into his dirty white vest. Harriet had stepped back and looked on in awestruck shock at what they had done.

The leader looked at me as if to complain about the unfairness of his treatment, the arm below his stabbed shoulder twitching at his side. The shotgun slipped from his grasp. The old cook screamed curses and planted her knife into his neck. Ibu Intan is quite short, so that long, sharp knife punched up. She drove it in, and it must have gone through his mouth and into his brain.

He raised his good arm to grab his neck but it batted hopelessly at the air. It was as if he could no longer fully control his arms and legs. Ibu Intan pulled the knife out again and stabbed his belly and chest in a frenzy, the motion pushing him out of the door on twitching legs until he toppled over. He wasn't dead yet, just jerking while I retched into the blood that was everywhere and Harriet tried to comfort me and turned her own attention from the miner's inevitable end. When I looked up, minutes later, Ibu Intan stood over him and her right hand dripped with his blood.

I ran from the hut to check on Rendy, certain that he was dead. The shotgun blast had been aimed badly and he was hurt more by his fall into the frame of the hall. He had bounced off several sharp-edged beams and was stabbed by exposed nails before he landed. We lifted him carefully and moved him towards the kitchen to inspect his injuries. How often I have thought about removing his shirt! I do not think anything is broken and he is not bleeding very much, but I fear that he may be concussed or have injuries we cannot see. I am not a doctor! We have a small supply of antibiotics to prevent infection. I hope that it is sufficient. He is unconscious but with rest and care he might yet survive, so we have moved him into my bedroom.

I hope that we are safe now, but we still have no way to get out of this evil place. Revo has lost so much blood that he cannot live much longer, although he is in Ibu Intan's care. I have done my best to clean Rendy's wounds and remove the small pellets near the surface, but many of them are too deep to dig out without causing him more harm. I can do nothing now but wait.

I will care for him as best I can. There is still a killer here with us. Cristian disliked Tara, and it is clear that Alison is mentally unstable. The two of them slaughtered the miners with absolute delight. And then there is Ibu Intan. Was that simply the rage of a mother protecting her family? The disappearance of Paul is suspicious, but he has been friendly with everyone. What if he is also dead? Who would kill such a gentle man?

* * *

I spent most of the day watching over Rendy. When I came out of my room this afternoon, everyone had gone except for myself and Ibu Intan and the injured and the dead. She has become obsessed by the idea of evil spirits in this place. Yesterday she even accused me of being a witch when we were in the forest. I told her that I do not believe in witches. She laughed and said that witches are not all monsters who live in the forest with the old tribes. I do not know what that means.

This terrible place took Bimo today, Revo is close to death, and I fear that I will become another of the broken-hearted when it takes my Rendy. I cannot take any pleasure in knowing that the river runs with the blood of those who would have killed us if we had not killed them. And if I do not live to be rescued, I hope that someone finds this diary so that the world will know that Rendy was a hero until the end.

Diary: Maya Pollard, night

Go to the jungle and help orangutans, they said. They did not say: burn a man alive and watch your new boyfriend chop two more to pieces. But then, they also didn't say that I'd get trapped in the jungle with a couple of nutters and a bunch of gangsters running an illegal mining operation. If I ever get back to the OST folks, I'm going to give them a free pass for the crazy that's happened here. Who could have seen all this coming?

On the positive side, I can now expand my CV with useful skills like 'built a barricade from junk' and 'took part in the successful defence of a remote camp against a deadly attack'. Employers love that kind of left-field stuff. It shows character.

I'm rambling, mainly because I'm feeling kind of chilled up here in the birdwatching tower with old Rangga. Haha, "old" Rangga. We're alive and it's fair to say we've been celebrating the fact because I don't think either of us expected to come through this. I know I should feel bad because of Bimo and Rendy and Revo, and those three guys I fucking burned to death, but I've just never felt so glad to be alive.

And Bimo, well he went out like a hero. A sneaky fucking hero but he took down two or three of those evil fuckers and scared the shit out of them too. Rendy too, but I hope he pulls through. Dewi won't give up on him. She adores that man, even if she won't tell anyone.

There's no fucking way I will ever forget the sounds those guys made when the fire came up around them. I hadn't even thought about what it would look like before I lit the little piece of bedsheet in front of me. It went up fast, shitloads faster than the line of fire you see in films. That was all I had to do and now I've killed three people. Well, technically Cris and Rangga killed them, but they were pretty fucked up. I don't know if it was the right thing to do but we couldn't help them and we couldn't leave them to die slowly. Is that still self-defence?

At least Rangga said something to the guy he finished off, and he was quick and clean about it. Not like Cris. I don't ever want to see anything like that again, the way Cris just drove the chainsaw right into the first guy and cut the injured one across the arm and chest. The miner fell on his back, and Cris was roaring like a viking as he chopped the guy's head off. There was so much fucking blood and I'm pretty sure Cris had an erection in those surfer shorts he wears. He smashed the chainsaw straight into the head of the second one of the burned guys and started looking for a way around the barricade to the miners who'd killed Bimo.

The only thing louder than Cris and his fucking chainsaw was Alison coming out at that miner and almost chopping his arm off with a parang. Shit!!!! That must be what she used to kill Paul. The fucking bitch!

And what they did to those miners on the jetty. They wanted to surrender but Alison hacked into them while Cris gutted them. The pair of them whooping and cheering and screeching gleefully. I'm not surprised the men in the boats left them behind. They took one quick look at Bimo to see he was dead and snogged furiously, both of them covered in blood. Sick fuckers.

The really sick shit, the thing I'm feeling really bad about, is that Rangga has never looked so fucking hot as he does to me now. I know he killed people too, but he was civilised compared to Cris and Alison. I should be scared of him but he makes me feel safe — he's not crazy like Cris, he's in control. I know he only did what he had to do, and he did it even though he didn't want to do it. He didn't just do it for himself, he did it for me and all the others, and if he hadn't been there I don't know what would have happened to us. Ever since we left the camp he's been telling me how bad he feels about killing people. I told him I was glad it was them, not us. It's not good, but it's true. He's such a Boy Scout and I find that sooo cute TBH.

It's wrong, I know, but this is all wrong. Everything that's happened. The thing I did today. I couldn't stand around afterwards and I knew he felt the same. I wanted to feel something different. Something good. He didn't argue when I led him away. He just looked at me with those gentle brown eyes full of sadness. When we got to the tower I made him look away and I put on the one nice top I was saving for meal with everyone before we fly home. I don't think I'm gonna need it now. I put on my little charm bracelet because I wanted to feel glamorous like we were going on, I don't know, a date or something. It's so dumb but I needed to feel normal for just a second.

Harriet was pretty pissed about us leaving her at the camp I think. Dewi's freaked out over Rendy, Ibu Intan's in the other room with Revo, and Alison took Cris off into the jungle. Those two had some crazy bloodlust shit going on. They scare me. I wasn't horny from the killing, not exactly, but it was either fuck Rangga or lose my shit. I shouldn't have to justify anything after what happened today. It doesn't make me a psycho like Cris and Alison.

Rangga's kind of quiet now, just smoking while I write and stroking my back. It's never been like that before with anyone. I've had fireworks and laughter before but this was different. None of that stuff but all of the tension, all my fear, it went out of me. It felt right. And good. I'm sure he felt the same thing. Even if it's just for now.

Now, though, we've got some food, a couple of sleeping bags and the shotgun. Rangga grabbed it where the miner's leader had dropped it outside Ibu Intan's room. I'd rather he had it than anyone else. I'd probably shoot my leg off and fuck knows what the two psychos would do with it. I guess we'll go back down tomorrow to see what's going on.

One last thing for tonight, cos I can't get it out of my head. Rangga told me what this is place is really called. Turns out Pondok Bahaya is Indonesian for Camp Danger. WTAF? He said it comes from something the forest people said when people like him came from Java. I didn't even know there were different kinds of people in Indonesia so I felt like stupid little white girl. Didn't tell him that, obvs. Anyway, everyone thought the Bahaya thing was a funny mistake, like they'd heard the wrong word. Now he's not so sure. No shit, Sherlock.

Photo: Maya Pollard

```
This selfie of Maya and Rangga was most probably
taken at the top of the birdwatching tower, where
there's a small enclosed area surrounded by a
```

panoramic walkway. The timestamp places it in the late afternoon.

They're both slightly grubby and topless, with the top of a sleeping bag covering them at the bottom of the picture, and bunched-up clothes under their heads. Maya is holding the phone, curled towards Rangga, who has one arm around her shoulders. If not happy, they appear united in defiance of the trials which they survived.

Email: Alan Caudwell to Imogen Nicholson

To: founder@saveorangutans.org.uk
From: alan@caudwell.org.uk
Subject: Pondok Bahaya diaries - August 1
Date: 2 September 2018 22:03

I am not sure what you will do, now that you know the fate of at least some of the staff and volunteers. I hope that your meeting with the authorities went to plan. I assume that Pak Rafi would have called if you had been arrested!

Whatever happened to Alison in the jungle, we have to accept that she and Cristian murdered at least one of the volunteers and several miners. I have very little enthusiasm for discovering Harriet's fate, but I don't want to let you down. I Googled this Rimadan that Alison believes has possessed her, but I can find nothing. I think it is a figment of her madness.

I know you said I should sleep, but after what I've read, I'm not sure I could. The sooner I get to the bottom of the rabbit hole, the sooner you can break me out for that dinner!

Alan x

Thursday, August 2, 2018

Diary: Dewi Rifqi, midday

I do not think my poor Rendy is healing. He has not woken for more than a few minutes since yesterday evening and he relieved himself in his sleep. I could not wake him. That was unfortunate.

A bruise stretches across his right side from the shoulder to the hip and I am certain that some of the wounds will become infected if he does not receive antibiotics. We do not have enough for both Revo and Rendy.

I have done my best to make him comfortable with the cushion my younger sister sewed for my graduation. It has orangutans on it, a mother and baby.

Ibu Intan spends most of her time in the next room with Revo, and she says only that he is sleeping. She woke me this morning so that we could watch over each other as we prepared hot water, rice and coffee, but I have not seen her since then and it is almost midday.

The camp is a mess but I do not have the strength to clear it on my own. The bodies of the miners still lie where they fell on the way from the jetty. I tried to move Bimo's body so that I could wrap it in a cloth but it was too heavy to lift. In the end I laid it as neatly as I could and laid a cloth over it, with bricks to weigh it down. They will not be needed for anything else now. I am sure that animals have already attacked the other bodies but I did not want to look too closely. I washed the miner's blood from the steps outside Revo's room. I know that most of it is inside and I hope that Ibu Intan has been able to clean it. There is a very bad smell outside the room. I do not know what she has done with the body.

Last night I heard noise from the office. I believe that Rangga and Maya slept there. The door was still shut this morning and I noticed that some items had gone from the kitchen area later on, but I heard nothing. I have been feeling very tired today, and it is possible that I slept deeply after my own breakfast. There seems to be little point in doing anything else.

It is many months since I learned that the forest is not to be feared if it is treated with caution, but I understand the risks of wild animals. There are no killers in the forest, only hunters and prey. In the human world there is evil, and that is truly frightening.

Diary: Maya, late afternoon

Me and Rangga decided to spend our daytime in the birdwatching tower where we can see anyone approaching us, but to sleep in the office because it has a lock on the door.

When I woke up this morning, he was looking at me and smiling. He smelled SO good, like earth and musk and cigarettes, which are just the best thing now, other than the sex. I probably just smelled of deet and sweat from last night but he still kissed me and said "Saya cinta kamu". It means "I love you" in Indonesian. Explaining it just made me want him more. Just for a minute, I forgot all the shit that put us in that cramped little bed, but then I banged my elbow on the wall :(The moment was gone, but I still wanted to say it back to him because I think I might mean it and even if I don't, he needs to feel it as much as I do.

I'd have stayed in there forever with him but it's not fair to leave Dewi on her own with Rendy and Ibu Intan. I don't think the old woman is all there.

Rendy looks kind of fucked with all those little black dots and bruises over his shoulder and chest from the shotgun, and more massive bruises where he fell down, but Rangga thinks he'll be OK if Dewi keeps cleaning his wounds. I don't know if he should be sleeping or not but it's probably good for him. It's not like we can make him stay awake. I gave her some bits from my little first aid kit but it's not much.

There's not much food, either. I mean, there's loads of rice and noodles and eggs and a few onions and stuff like tomato sauce and sugar, but not many vegetables. There's a lot of porridge, too. I will never eat porridge again if I get out of here. We haven't got much fresh water left and the only other option is to boil the river water. At least there's a pipe to pump it from the river. If it rains again we can get water fresh out of the sky.

I didn't see Revo. Ibu Intan came out to help us cook and she told Dewi that he was still sleeping but he wasn't getting any worse. She wouldn't let us in to see him. Dewi asked about the body of the leader and Ibu Intan said not to worry about it. Rangga looked kinda surprised but he shrugged and didn't ask for details. When Dewi explained to me, I felt the same.

I had something more important to tell Dewi - the blood on the floor of my old room. We all went to look at it and I think we all know that Alison and Cris killed Paul. I'm sure it was Alison who attacked Tara. The trouble is, no-one has seen Harriet since yesterday and we're all thinking the same thing: they've killed her too. She wouldn't have stayed away for this long.

Who knows where they've gone and when they'll come back?

I found Alison's diary. It looks — insane is the only word — scrawled all over with mad drawings of jungle animals and people fucking. I'm going to read it tonight. Maybe it'll tell us WTF is wrong with her.

Rangga wants to kill them and I know it's wrong, but I'm scared and he's the only one who can protect us now. I'm not tough and I don't think I could take on crazy Alison, let alone Cris. I liked him <u>because</u> he was big and muscular. Yeah, maybe I should be rethinking my choices.

Dewi said Ibu Intan went crazy when that miner broke into their room, but I don't think she could stop Ali and Cris.

Dewi and Rangga said we should move the bodies before they start to smell or attract animals. That might be worse than the crazies coming for us. Dewi had already wrapped up Bimo so we put him in the room where Paul and Cris slept. Paul's stuff is all still in there. I took his diary, too. It felt like the right thing to do. We might have to put Revo and Rendy in there soon. I don't want to think about it. What a fucking mess. They deserve a proper burial when we're rescued.

There are too many miners to wrap up and carry to the rooms. The ground is too hard and full of roots to dig graves. Rangga said we should burn them or throw them in the river. I said throw them in the river. Dewi wasn't happy but she agreed it's best. Me and Dewi both retched while we were wrapping the burned bodies and carrying them down the hill. I think Rangga went off to vom in the forest later. There are some old concrete bricks so we rolled and pushed them down the hill and tied them to the miners to stop them floating. Rangga's worried the bodies will attract crocodiles if they don't sink fast. He said the river's a lot deeper than you'd think. It took all afternoon to have them all lined up on the dock. Rangga said a few words I didn't understand and we pushed them in one by one. The sheets were full of air and I thought they wouldn't sink but they soon got wet and disappeared.

Watching them go under the water, I couldn't help thinking that could be me. I could really, actually, literally die here. If it wasn't for Rangga I probably would be dead already. I'm just a student from Surrey who wanted to see some orangutans. I don't know any Bear Grylls jungle survival crap. If I don't starve or get malaria or something, there's a couple of fucking psychos running around in the jungle. Tara would know what to do. I don't have a Scooby.

We had to get clean after we'd moved the bodies, so the three of us took turns standing outside the shower block while we washed. You could see there was blood in there already. Wonder if it was from Paul or Harriet?

Now I'm in the tower with Rangga. Just for a few hours. It's the only place I really feel safe.

Dewi said Ibu Intan was saying all this weird shit about ghosts and it was freaking her out. She looks so scared. I forget she's only a couple of years older than me. She's going to lock Rendy and herself in with water and food and stay quiet until she hears from us. We'll stay in the office again tonight. Rangga said he'd try to start the generator to get us some more light and charge a phone for some music. The power hasn't been on since before the miners came. We used a lot of petrol on the barricade, but if we're careful there'll be enough to last a few days, he says.

I feel safe up here in the tower, though. Just having Rangga nearby with the shotgun. Knowing I can hold him tonight. Maybe we can get through until somebody comes to get us. Maybe.

Wish I knew what those two fucking nutters were doing.

Diary: Maya, evening

What the fuck is wrong with Ali? What the actual fuck?

Tara? Paul? And you think you're what, possessed? I tried telling Rangga about it and he gets the basics that she killed them but how do I tell him about Rimadan or whatever you think it is? I want to talk to Dewi but it's too fucking late to go outside now.

Rangga just thinks Ali's fucking batshit and he wants to protect me which is a hundred kinds of adorable and any other time it would make me kind of horny but I'm so scared of those two now. I want to push every cupboard and cabinet against the door until it's light again.

Fuck.

And the sex. I'm not like a prude or anything, obvs — FFS I like sex!!! — but she was writing porn to this Manny guy while she was gagging for Cris to see her. I was only having fun. If she'd told me she was that thirsty for Cris I would have stopped flirting. So maybe I did go on about him a bit at first but fucking hell she must have been flicking the bean 10 times a night.

The drawings are just weird. They freak me out. The jungle's alive with all the trees laughing. She's so cock-obsessed it's almost funny. Then you see what they're doing. And then — I didn't know whether to laugh or gag — I saw my face and my tats and I don't know if that's a person or an animal. Does she think I'd do that with whatever the fuck that thing is? Does she have fantasies about it?

I want to go home.

Friday, August 3, 2018

Diary: Dewi Rifqi, afternoon

Maya showed me Alison's diary this morning. She thought I would know what this Rimadan is, but I am a city girl from Java. I know nothing about these backward people. Alison is simply crazy. There are no jungle spirits. The only spirit is my God. And some of the things that woman has drawn, I shiver to remember them. I think that Maya even hid the worst from me.

Ibu Intan has become like a mother to Rendy and I, and I think that she approves of me caring for Rendy as a wife would to a sick husband. Her soup is having a miraculous effect on his recovery. He sleeps still but the colour has returned to his skin and he seems to be more comfortable. When he wakes he is very sleepy but more lucid and less in pain. I do not know what she puts in the soup but she forages for special ingredients and she has told me not to drink it because it will make me sleep also.

I asked Ibu Intan if she had heard of Rimadan. She did not recognise the name, but I described the ghostly clouded leopard of which Alison wrote. She said that her grandmother was a Dayak nomad and she talked of other tribes that had hunters with animal spirit companions which taught them the way of the forest. They had to be sated with the flesh of a fresh kill and her grandmother used to scare them with stories of the hunters taking naughty children into the forest and eating them.

Now Ibu Intan is convinced that we must leave because Alison and Cristian are serving an animal spirit. She is certain that they will kill and eat us if we stay.

The only spirit is my God. I do not believe this story but if Alison believes it, it does not matter. No one has seen Harriet or Paul for days. If Alison and Cris are killing people then we must leave. I will talk to Maya and Rangga when they return. I pray that Rendy is able to walk tomorrow. We cannot delay.

Diary: Maya Pollard, night

We're getting out of here tomorrow. Dewi told Ibu Ints about Ali's animal ghost and she knew what it was. She was frightened.

They had a big debate with Rangga in Indonesian. I didn't get much of it but everyone wants to leave in the morning.

Ibu Ints thinks Ali's possessed and Rangga and Dewi think she's just mad. As for Cris…I'll never forget the look on his face with that chainsaw. And the hard-on after he killed those men. Fuck!

Good news is that Rendy looks a lot better. Ibu Ints says he should wake up tomorrow. Good enough to walk, she promised.

Bad news is that Revo's dead. The old woman had wrapped him up but she couldn't move him. We did it together. Only dropped him a couple of times. Rangga was a bit pissed at that. Dead people are so heavy!

I just felt numb when Dewi passed it on. He was always smiley but I didn't know him and now he's just another dead guy. I've seen so many bodies now. Gotta face it...Paul and Harriet are dead bodies now...somewhere in the jungle. Poor old fuckers.

I don't know where we'll go tomorrow. Rangga says the mining camp should be almost empty now. I want to go down the river but he said we'll get stuck if it's still blocked. Guess he's right. Miners must have a sat phone.

Email: Imogen Nicholson to Alan Caudwell

To: alan@caudwell.org.uk
From: foundor@saveorangutans.org.uk
Subject: Re: Pondok Bahaya diaries - August 2-3
Date: 3 September 2018 00:33

I am appalled beyond words. I would not have allowed either Cristian or Alison within a thousand miles of Pondok Bahaya if I had known they would behave like that.

This Rimadan thing. Ghost, demon, spirit, whatever it is. Does Alison really think she's possessed? I don't know whether I should consult a shrink or a shaman. Perhaps I need to speak to both.

As for Cristian, I think he has always been a monster. The things we're hearing about him get worse every day.

I had to stop reading, have a stiff drink before I could go on. It feels like the whole world is upside-down.

Jenny x

DESTRUCTION

Saturday, August 4, 2018

Diary: Maya Pollard, afternoon

Fuck! Fuck! FUCK!!!! I've got to keep moving. They could be looking for me now. They know about the tower. I need to write this now, in case it's the last thing I get to say.

Fucking Cris and that mad bitch Alison. They were waiting for us. Jesus, I wasn't imagining anything yesterday. Someone WAS following us.

Rangga had the boat in the water and he was holding it for us when that spear took his leg. It wasn't the spear that killed him, though.

It's only luck that I got away. I was halfway down the hill, in the trees, carrying bags and water and food. Dewi and Ibu Ints were behind me helping Rendy. He was awake but he's still weak. Is? Was? Fuck!

Someone came at them. I think it was Alison. She was so caked in dirt that I could hardly see her face but I'd know those crazy eyes anywhere. Ibu Ints let go of Rendy and pulled out one of those kitchen knives Dewi says she used on the miners' boss.

She ran at her, screaming "Rimadan!" and something in Indonesian.

Ali had a spear. My brain flipped. It's still flipping at the picture of naked Alison covered in shit with the wildest eyes I've ever seen, sticking a spear into Ibu Ints. The old woman stopped dead and fell silent. Alison looked surprised and delighted that the spear had worked.

She pulled the spear out and stabbed Ibu Ints again. The old woman dropped her knife and grabbed her belly where the blood was running out. When the spear hit her the second time, she just fell over.

I think that's when Dewi screamed and I ran to the boat, falling down the bank past the dock. Cris barrelled past me and threw a spear at Rangga. He'd lifted his head at Dewi's scream but he couldn't move fast enough.

He staggered and his leg went out from underneath him. The spear was all the way through his thigh on one side. Blood running down his leg. He tried to stand up but the spear got in the way so he just thrashed about turning the rusty water bright red. I could feel myself start to scream his name. What happened next stopped the scream dead in my throat.

Something huge came out of the river. The world stopped. A dark green torpedo of muscle and teeth grabbed Rangga in jaws as long as his leg. The spear splintered around him, he flipped on his back and SPLASH he was gone. He didn't even scream. I saw Cris, transfixed by the crocodile. He hadn't seen me. I ran. I should have helped Dewi and Rendy but I ran. I kept running until my lungs ached and had to stop. I took one deep breath, remembered what I'd seen and I started puking. I thought I'd done with vomit by now, but no.

Rangga Bayhacki. That was his name. I don't even really know if that's how to spell it. He was just this nice, hot funny older guy I was making friends with and then we were lovers and I just wanted to get away from here so we could be together. I know he's got a family but right here and now we had something. He wanted to be with me too. I'm sure. Oh God, his poor family. This is all so wrong. I don't know what to do next.

I think those guys will leave me out here until I get hungry and try to steal something from the camp. I dropped everything when I ran off. All I've got is a little backpack with the diaries, my headlight, my phone, a half-charged battery pack, a first aid kit and some clean underwear. Clean pants. I've got my priorities all right there. Nothing worth shit to survive on but I'll die in clean knickers. My mum would be proud. I don't even have a knife to defend myself. Like I know how. If there was a loaf of white sliced I could make a sandwich and that's about it.

I'm going to have to sleep in the tower, if I can even sleep with those two around. It's so obvious but I can't think of anywhere else. I am so fucked. How long can I last out here? Longer than Dewi and Rendy will, that's for sure. Fuck. Fuck fuck fuck fuck fuck.

Diary: Tara Fowler, evening

This entry in Tara's diary is written in a heavier hand, and the pages are dirtier.

What the fuck has been happening here? I spend a few days away from the camp and Alison turns into a fucking cannibal? I would have walked right into it if I hadn't found Harriet's body on the viewing platform. Or what's left of it. Shit. I should have walked downriver, I knew it. So here I am, stuck in a tower with a terrified girl and no food. God, I'm so hungry. Even after finding that mess.

I thought it was animals at first, even when I saw Cristian and Alison's clothes on the platform. But that body wasn't either of them and that wasn't their blood. What have they done? Alison wasn't right from the day we arrived and Cristian's been nothing but trouble. I always give people a chance but WTF is wrong with them?

I could hardly describe it to Maya without wanting to be sick or crying. I want to describe it. I have to. They'd carved into Harriet's body. It was like they'd been trying to draw things on her skin. She was sunburned like they'd laid her out for hours and bitten like the bugs had been at her all night. Her lips were puffed up even though they'd gone pale when she died. She must have suffered for hours and hours and hours.

And chunks had been cut off her. Her legs. Her arse. Was she even dead when they did that? There was even a fire. I think they cooked her. I don't know how much they ate, but I have to assume they did it. Fucking sickos.

I hid near the viewing platform until it was almost dark. Not too close. By the time I got there, there were flies on the body. I don't know what eats dead things in the rainforest, but I didn't want to be around when it got there.

Then I crept up to the camp as near as I dared. It wasn't hard to find with all the screaming from Rendy and Dewi and the laughing from Alison and Cristian. I wanted to run in and help them but I'm so hungry and weak. The pair of them were stalking around what's left of the hall. It's just a frame now with half a roof and bits of planks on the wall in some places. There's a fire in the middle. I wouldn't be surprised if they burn the whole place down.

It took me a minute to make out Rendy and Dewi tied to posts in the middle with their clothes torn off. Then I saw all the heads on spears. Revo, Bimo, Ibu Intan and Paul. All dead. I hope they didn't suffer like Harriet. I don't think they did now I've talked to Maya. But Harriet. I can't stop thinking about the state of her body. She must have been in agony.

***

They're doing the same to Dewi and Rendy now. Alison was cutting Dewi with a knife and talking to her. Dewi was screaming and sobbing and Rendy was begging them to stop. Every time she screamed, they screamed with her and told her to scream more. I didn't want to stay too long in case they saw me, and when Cristian started on Rendy while Alison taunted Dewi, I had to leave. I couldn't take any more.

I thought I could hide in the birding tower so I crept around the back of the dormitories and retched in the forest when I thought I was out of sight, then I made it to the tower. I almost fell off the ladder when I saw Maya up here with a stick in her hand, ready to knock me back down. I was so happy to see her and the expression on her face, seeing someone she must have thought was drowned. For a minute I thought I was going to start giggling, I felt like I was going mad, then everything I'd seen and done washed over me and the relief I felt at seeing one person who was happy to see me…I couldn't climb the ladder until my tears stopped.

Maya's filled me in on what happened here after I fell into the river. I guess I should count myself lucky that she collected all the diaries she could find. If I'm going to leave something behind from this, I should explain how I ended up back in this nightmare.

**

Alison must have intended to push me into the water. The shock of it woke me up but all I could feel was the current pulling me under the water. I was fighting to swim up, my lungs were bursting and somehow I came up on the other side of the trees. I splashed about on the surface until I got my breath, but I was caught in a current and I couldn't see the boat. I started to think about snakes and crocodiles and I knew I had to get out of the river.

I saw one of those wooden houses on stilts that never seem to have anyone in them. I swam as hard as I could and grabbed the stilts to catch my breath. Everything was hurting from the other night but I knew I wasn't going to die if I could pull myself out. My boots were weighing me down but I didn't want to lose them. I thought they'd never come off but I tied the laces together and hung them round my neck. I haven't done that since I was a teenager in a swimming pool. It's a lot harder when your ribs are bruised.

There was a bit of a ladder at the back and I very slowly moved round until I could grab it. The stilts were only a metre or two apart but it felt like 100m every time. I came so close to dropping those damned boots. I thought my arms would stop working, but I got up one rung at a time until I flopped onto that platform and crashed out.

I must have passed out for a couple of hours, but in the end I dragged myself into the house and found a grotty old bed where I zonked out again. I took off my clothes to dry them out and saw leeches clamped to my legs and arms. I couldn't do anything except wait until they fell off. I remembered Rendy telling me that you could get infected if you tried to pull leeches off, and they didn't hurt. It was all too hard.

The next morning the leeches were gone. I found a jar on the deck that had water in it from the storm so I drank that. I still had so many aches and bruises from where I had been kicked, but it felt like nothing was broken.

There was no more water and I didn't fancy hanging off the ladder to fill that jar, so I convinced myself I would have to find help. I was on the same side of the river as our camp, so I decided to come back. Now I wish I'd gone down the river and tried to find another house that still had some people in it, but you can't spend your life wondering what might have been.

The house had a walkway on stilts that went into the jungle. My clothes were still damp but when is anything really dry out here? I found an empty plastic bottle and filled it near the shore. I strained the worst of the dirt through my T-shirt. It wasn't clean but I had to drink, even if it made me sick. I feel fine so far.

I guessed that Rendy hadn't been able to get through the block on the river and then it hit me — they probably all thought I was dead. No one was coming for me. I'd have to get out of there on my own. There were two choices: find a village down the river or go back to Pondok Bahaya.

When we hit that debris, we were still at least half a day from the nearest village that I could remember. What was I going to do, make a boat?

No, but I've done marathons and Tough Mudders. I put up with that arsehole boyfriend and all his threats. We'd only gone a few miles downstream from PB. I thought, it'll be a tough hike but all I have to do is follow the river.

I know it's mad, but I enjoyed it some of the time. I love the mornings in camp, when you can smell the jungle waking up in the sun, but this was even more intense. Every breath felt like new life, even when it hurt. I could taste nature. Nothing came too near me with my heavy boots. I didn't surprise anything that might bite me, either, but I heard the little forest deer and monkeys chattering in the trees. I even saw an orangutan watching me from high up one morning when I woke up in a tree. Last year Rendy and Ibu Intan showed me a few fruits I could eat, so I didn't starve but had to stop for some painful shits. That might be the water though.

It was slow going. After a few hours I had to come away from the river because the storm had made everything boggy. There were some steep banks and slimy rocks where I scraped my fingertips and fell on my arse. As if it wasn't bruised enough! I had to climb into a tree every night, and that's not easy withou orangutan arms or leopard claws. The orangutans would hav laughed at my nests.

I found a stick to help me walk and somehow I ploughed thinking of how great it would be to see Rendy and Harriet Paul and everyone when I got back. I got better at finding my even when I was tired, and one time I started to think I mig walking around in circles because everything looked the bloody same, so at the end of every day I went downhill until I found the river. It slowed me down but I knew where I was, sort of.

I stumbled over a stake in the ground this afternoon and suddenly I knew I was close because it was where we planted trees last year. Then I got to the path and followed it to the platform. That's when I found Harriet, or what's left of her. Christ, I threw up then.

※ ※ ※

So here I am.

We need to get out of here. I've been marching on hope for the last few days and now it's all gone. I've got bruises on top of the bruises from the attack. Guess I didn't have a broken rib, or I wouldn't have made it this far. Pretty sure at least one of my cuts is infected, even after Maya used up her antiseptic wipes.

Maya says the boat's still where Rangga left it by the water. If we can get in it without being eaten by a crocodile we can float away and work out how to start the motor when we're on the river. It can't be that hard. Maya says Rangga probably put the shotgun 'own in the boat. I bet those mad fuckers don't even know it's ·re. It might help us when we get up the river.

Rendy and Dewi aren't going to keep those two psychos busy ore than a day or two. We can't rescue them. I know we try, but all that time in the jungle will be for nothing if we some help. Alison and Cristian don't know I'm here so ibly think they can just wait for Maya to try and get ⁻uck them!!!!

't's really stupid, but I couldn't help getting angry It's never going to be finished. When I first met me how much he wanted to improve the facilities summer was the start of his big project. He was so ducation centre in the heart of the rainforest. Now lie there.

Diary: Maya Pollard, evening

TARA IS HERE!!!! I don't normally do the crazy caps lock thing but OMG I'm not alone and she's not dead. I mean, she looks like shit and I haven't got enough wet wipes and antibac gel for all those cuts, but she can walk and talk and we've got a fucking plan to get away. If only she'd come with biscuits.

She told me about Harriet. Poor old lady. She was so sweet to me. And to Ali. That bitch is crazy AF.

It's weird that Tara and me didn't get on because of Cris and now we're both terrified he'll try to carve us up and eat us while we're alive.

I don't want to think about what they're doing to Rendy and Dewi. Tara told me about Rendy and how she turned him down. She feels bad but she shouldn't. It was just a shock and after all she'd been through with that prick at home he should have waited. Men are fucking idiots sometimes. I told her how much I'd started to like Rangga and how I was scheming ways to come back here and see him or stay with him or something before it all went to shit. She looked kind of shocked but then she just smiled and hugged me and said she was sorry he was dead. I didn't tell her we had sex the night before he died. Not really the time to be so extra.

※ ※ ※

Had to stop there for a minute. I miss him already. I only knew him for a few days. I'll never be able to explain what he was like. Other women my age will think I'm weird for wanting to go with some old Indonesian guy but in the end he was everything I wanted and I'll always know I found him. At the very least his kids should know he was a hero.

I'm just going to sit and watch the forest now. We're getting out of here tomorrow.

Sunday, August 5, 2018

Diary: Tara Fowler, morning

Tara's writing is more relaxed here, although the pages have a few water marks splashed across them.

We got out. I can hardly believe it. The boat was exactly where Maya said Rangga had left it when the croc took him, floating in the shallows. We got up before dawn and went slowly around the edge of the camp, but we could see the two crazies sleeping in the middle, wrapped up in each other. I don't know if Rendy and Dewi were alive or dead. We couldn't help them anyway. I didn't know Dewi that well but she was a sweet girl. She'd be better off dead than alive with those two. I don't want to think about what they were doing to him last night, but Rendy is probably dead now. I just hope he didn't suffer. He was one of the good guys.

We let the boat drift downstream for a while before we tried to start the engine. I've seen the camp staff do it a few times, and it started on the third try. I think the noise woke Cristian and Alison — as we went past I could hear shouting, but Maya said it will take them a few hours to get the other boat into the water and they'll have to put petrol in it. If they even know how. She's driving now, and we're going slowly in case we see a fisherman's house or somewhere else we could hide instead of going to the mine camp. Maya thinks there were only two men left in the boats after they attacked. I don't think they'll be pleased to see us.

We found the shotgun and a bag of shells — is that right? — in the bottom of the boat after we started the engine. I shot clay pigeons once. We'll just have to look like we know what we're doing and try not to shoot each other. There's a parang, too. It must be Rangga's. Maya tried not to cry as she picked it up.

The river is peaceful. I could almost forget we're stuck here and just watch the birds and monkeys like it was a normal summer volunteer trip. The sun is up and we're just having a nice time on the river. Yeah, right!

※ ※ ※

SHIT!!! There was nowhere else to stop and there's someone in the mining camp and they've seen us. It might just be one person. Maya keeps looking at me like I should have a clue. I'm just as lost as you now, girl. The miners are probably dangerous, but we know Alison and Cristian <u>only</u> want to hurt us. We can't go back.

Diary: Maya Pollard, evening

I don't know if I'll sleep any better here than I did in that fucking tower. These miners are the same fuckers who were in the boats when their mates came to kill us. They know what happened. They're not going to call for help. They must know the river's blocked. They're just acting nice to keep us here. Two tired women with nowhere to go.

Tara looks shattered. I dunno, I probably look like shit too. FFS I haven't had a wash for a week or eaten proper food. I think the last time I ate properly was before the old lady turned out to be a crazy cannibal witch. After that it's just been biscuits and random fruit. Tara's been drinking river water and eating fruit off the trees for a week so she's even worse than me. We both smell like shit.

It felt like hours getting here and then we sat in the boat watching the miners' camp. We talked ourselves round in stupid circles, wondering what to do and if Alison and Cris were going to come up the river any moment or the the engine wouldn't start again. In the end it was a choice of going back to definitely murdery or just probably murdery with a chance of rapey too. At least the second one has food and fresh water. Maybe even a shower. We just have to stay together and watch out for each other. Get our strength back.

The two men must have heard the engine cos they came running to the dock when we got here. They must have thought we were coming to get them from down the river and when they saw us they looked properly fucked off. They shouted at us in Indonesian and we had to make them slow right down just so Tara could get a few words in. She waved the shotgun at them and they stepped back while we got off the boat. I held the parang and tried to look mean. We said we wanted a phone and food and a place to sleep. They talked to each other until Tara waved the gun at them again and then they showed us into a long wide wooden hall with a few long tables and dirty plates and cups everywhere. Guess it's their canteen. These guys don't tidy up for themselves.

One of them went away and came back with two bowls of rice and hot tea with that sweet milk they drink here. It could have been drugged or whatever but we were both so hungry we didn't care. We made them sit at the other end of the room and took turns holding the gun and eating.

Tara asked for the phone again but they shrugged and said "no phone". Guess there's no phone here. Then they showed us to this bedroom in another hut on stilts. Everything's on stilts a few feet above the ground here. It's just mud underneath but there are weird coloured streams running through it. Some sort of chemical shit I guess. It all smells like burning plastic.

Anyway, even though it's basically a wooden hut, the room's got a sink and towels, a bolt[12] on the door and two beds. A sink with running water though! An electric light! It feels like a hotel lol!!! I wonder who lived here? For all I know, I burned them alive on Wednesday.

We made the men walk away and pushed a bed against it after we locked it. I don't know what we'll do later. There's windows at the back and there's a few gaps in the wood so we can see if anyone's at the door.

I think it's only just after midday, but as soon as I saw a bed I knew I could sleep.

We had to help each other wash because we were so filthy. We've both got so many bruises and bites now, it was like walking on glass to try and get clean without hurting each other. Having my hair washed though. Soooooo good. Even with crappy cheap soap it feels the best. We're both red from all day on the river but we found some vaseline in a washbag. Not exactly Nivea but it feels good. Vaseline! Not judging a dead man. Sure it gets lonely here. Clean clothes too! Well, kind of clean clothes from whoever was here before. It's a shame Indonesian guys are all so skinny. I don't want to show any skin when we go outside in front of those creeps. The only thing that fitted me was a Liverpool football strip but the shorts are way too tight on my bum and the T-shirt is too clingy everywhere. Red's not really my colour. Two days ago I was showing off my bod to Rangga. Now I feel naked in a T-shirt.

Tara's taller than most Indonesian men I've seen. She's kind of muscly and she's got big boobs so in the end she found a baggy hoodie and sweatpant shorts. The hoodie's got a stupid "I heart

---

[12] Maya had written "lock" and scrubbed it out here.

LDN" thing on it but I'm kind of jealous: it looks soooo cosy. I feel scared and cold inside all the time.

I'm sitting on the bed by the window while Tara gets the first sleep. She was out before she'd finished telling me that she was too scared to sleep.

Diary: Tara Fowler, night

This entry is far more hurried and difficult to read, confirming that it was written in poor light. The last line is a scribble that took some time to decipher.

I don't trust these two men but at least they let us clean up, eat and rest. They probably think they can sneak in while we're sleeping. They're probably right. I could sleep for days. Maya looked so scared and tired before she went to sleep. I wish I could say something but we're both thinking the same about those men and what they want. If I write it will help me to stay awake while Maya's asleep. The fear isn't enough to keep us going any more.

Some of my bruises are actually going down. It looks like Maya's antibac stopped my cuts getting infected. I should be full of worms and god knows what by now. There was a first aid kit in the room with a bunch of alcohol wipes in it. I feel better now, just so raw. And some paracetamol. My head's aching a bit less anyway now I've slept on something more comfortable than a wooden floor or a tree branch. This hoodie's like a hug. I almost feel warm inside. Almost.

We've turned the light off so it looks like we're sleeping, but they have a lot of floodlights around the camp so I can see pretty well. I want to save Maya's head torch for emergencies. There are lights on in some of the other huts so I think there might be more people here, but I haven't seen anyone outside except the same two men. Something tells me they didn't cook the rice and tea we had before. Maybe there's someone here cooking for them, like Ibu Intan?

I've had time to think about what happened before I was attacked. I feel like such a bitch now for turning Rendy down like that. Right now I would kill to have that solid little body snuggled up next to me and his warm, calm voice telling me we'll work it out. He always had another idea, a way of looking at things from a different angle. And he loved the rainforest and the wildlife. He was strong and gentle and peaceful at the same time. But he came up with the plan to fight the miners and it worked!

I was just so surprised by him. I couldn't see how he would fit into my world, but…what is my world? A house with no-one in it. A phone I'm scared to answer. What if my world was his world? Wouldn't that be an adventure? That's what Maya said about Rangga. Everything about it was wrong on the surface but if he was the right guy for her then that was enough. Why should we think everyone would want to come and be part of our world in our rainy little country, and leave behind everything they know? I was such an arrogant little white girl. Who would leave behind a world like this?

I'll never know. Rendy's dead now. I hope he is, for his sake. And Dewi too. Maya told me how Dewi was caring for Rendy and now I think of the way she looked at him, it was so obvious. Poor girl. I hope he never…[13]

Photo: Tara and Maya

```
This is one of the last photos taken by anyone in
the group.
    It's a selfie of Tara and Maya in their room at
the mining camp, wearing the ill-fitting clothes
```

---

[13] The sentence ends abruptly here, as though Tara was interrupted.

taken from the room's former occupiers. Behind them is a single bed across a door, with men's clothes and other personal items strewn across it.

Both women have bags under their eyes, Tara's black eye and split lip are still visible, and Maya has a couple of scratches on her face, but they're both clean. Their smiles and Maya's ironic V-sign are at odds with the fear in their eyes.

Monday, August 6, 2018

Diary: Maya Pollard, early morning

> This diary entry is smudged with palm-prints that look like both dirt and blood, and splashed with water. The writing is hurried but marked with pauses where she has finished a sentence and overwritten the last letter, last word or a piece of punctuation before launching into the next sentence.

When I was a first year at uni, I got properly off my head on shrooms and had one of those conversations with my best mate about whether the world is real or just a simulation or a dream or something. This feels like that. The camp and the river and the rainforest don't feel like places I came to by getting on a plane, and then another plane and a boat — it feels more like I went to sleep and I only think I woke up, but I'm still in a dream that just feels like the real world. I don't mean it's like a lucid dream where you can control it, because I DON'T feel like I have control over anything except myself. Or what if I'm just a character in a game like The Sims, and someone just took me out of one simulation and put it in another without erasing my memories? I know people who do fucked up things to their people in The Sims.

I've killed six people this week. I had to do it because they wanted to hurt me, but I'm not a killer. Only now I am. I'm, like, a totally different person to the person I was a week ago. Is that what happened to Alison? Did she just wake up and decide it didn't matter if she started killing people? So yeah, last night was crazy shit. I mean, technically we might have killed more people now than Alison and Cristian. I didn't enjoy it but I did it, so what the fuck?

I thought maybe we were going to be safe. It's not hard to work out what they wanted from us. Rangga said the only women who come up to the camps are expected to do everything the miners want. I don't just mean cooking, cleaning, and washing clothes. Local girls don't do it. That's why that guy lost it at Bimo. It's like the WORST thing a woman can do. Most of the women aren't Indonesian. They're brought here from Thailand or Burma or Vietnam. I don't think they all get a choice about it.

By the time I woke Tara for my turn to sleep it was almost dark and we agreed to just take turns through the night. I think we've both got used to being hungry. That rice was the first decent food we'd both had for days. I don't know how long it was, but I had two more little sleeps and a piss in a bucket before they tried to force the door. Tara was awake so the first thing I heard was her whispering to me to wake up. There was a bit of light from the moon and the lights around the camp because they keep a generator running all night.

We could hear both of them outside and Tara pointed at the window on the far side of the room. The windows were on a hinge so we grabbed our bags to get away and jumped. My head was just like buzzing with excitement and I was scared but this time it felt familiar, like we knew what we were doing now. As if!

The ground under the window was muddy and we both ended up covered in shit but the miners were making a noise now, banging on the door and shouting.

I didn't even think about all the cak we were slipping in. We just ran away from the river to where the buildings were dark. They were all locked but we could hide and look around at the one we'd come from. The banging and shouting got louder and then there was a crash and more shouting while they pushed the bed out of the way. The light came on and they must have worked out what we'd done. Rangga taught me a few tasty words in Indonesian and I heard them all. We were not going to be treated nicely when they found us, but we'd have to go past them to get back to the boat.

Tara said we'd just have to try to lose them around the buildings in the dark and double back. I didn't have any better ideas and on the plus side they were noisy and angry and we were quiet, so maybe we could do it.

There was another room with lights on, like ours but bigger. We should have stayed away but there were female voices coming from it and a radio playing some squeaky Asian pop music. We were so scared again and there had to be someone who would help us. Besides I was already starting to feel lost and I'm not sure Tara was too sure either. It wasn't like our camp where everything went downhill to the river and there are just like four buildings.

We poked our heads up to one of the screen windows like a couple of meerkats and saw three women. Two of them were about my age or maybe younger, the other a bit older, maybe about Tara's age. They weren't dressed in much for women in this part of the world, like no headscarves and just vests and skirts, and both the younger women had bruises on their arms. They didn't look happy, not exactly, but they were chatting and the older woman was tidying up some plates and cooking stuff. I suddenly felt very hungry again.

We needed to stay out of sight and they might be able to hide us. The smell of their food might have influenced us both. We hadn't eaten since lunch and my stomach growled at the smell of something frying.

We couldn't see the miners, so Tara went around to the front and knocked on the door. The older woman opened it and rattled out something in Indonesian. It didn't sound friendly, but when Tara said "Help! Please!" in English she looked us up and down and waved us in then shut the door in a hurry. I had the shotgun wrapped in a towel in my bag. I didn't want to freak them out if they were helping us.

The younger women pointed at our clothes and giggled about something — I think they were talking about the men who used to own them and the way our tops fit us. Or don't. I wrapped my arms around my chest.

The older woman said something sharp and they got us some water to drink while she scooped some rice and vegetables out of a pan. We both said thanks but the boss woman didn't seem to have anything more to say to us and told one of the younger women to wipe up our muddy footprints. She gave off a vibe that was half mother and half prison warden. One of my old school friends has a super-strict mum who never let us in the house. That was how it felt between those three.

One of the younger ones introduced herself. She was Soetanto, her friend was Pleun. They were both pretty, more Chinese than Indonesian and definitely younger than me, but Pleun had bruises on her face and arms. Fresh ones and big old purple splotches. The older woman was Nirmala. No bruises on her. It was obvious she was in charge of the younger women. Soetanto spoke a little English, enough that we knew to hide when the men knocked at the door. I guess he asked Nirmala if she'd seen us. The woman said no and the men went away. They were very agitated but she was clearly a good bullshitter.

Soetanto gave us a towel and we tried to wipe some of that nasty mud off each other. It smelled really grim. The room had more beds than people, so we gladly sat on empty beds and wolfed down the bowls. As soon as it hit my belly I felt super tired again. I thought it would be OK to sleep because Nirmala had lied to the men about us. We should have taken turns again but I couldn't fight it any more. I think Tara was the same. We weren't thinking straight. We must have both crashed out.

The next thing I felt was something very cold at my throat. Soetanto was kneeling in front of me and she said she was sorry but Nirmala had decided that it was better to give us to the men now than wait for them to find out about us. She said that it would mean that she and Pleun would just be able to do the good things. She didn't want to do the bad things any more. She was very very sorry but she was stuck here and now we were too. Nirmala was behind me, holding the knife around my throat. I tried to turn but I could only see Pleun standing next to Nirmala and that knife felt very sharp. Where could they go anyway? I'm not even sure the two of them know where they are. I couldn't find us on a map of Borneo. I bet they didn't have passports or anything. I don't have a passport any more. Shit.

I was about to give in when there was a grunt. Nirmala's hand went loose. Soetanto looked horrified and happy at the same time. Nirmala made a weird deflating noise. When I turned round she was on the floor and Tara was sitting on the bed behind her with the parang in her hand. There was blood from the tip almost to the handle. I don't know how she got it out of her bag without them hearing, maybe the radio covered it and if Soetanto saw her, she didn't say anything.

The knife was in front of me and I grabbed it. Pleun screamed and started shouting for the men. Soetanto begged her to be quiet but she was so scared she wouldn't stop. I told Tara we had to shut her up but I couldn't attack a scared girl younger than me.

I could never have imagined that look of cold resolve on Tara's face. Pleun was still kneeling behind me and screaming. Tara's not super-tall but she towered over that girl with the parang pressed to her throat. She asked her to stop but she just screamed louder. Tara said she was sorry, she pushed, and the screaming stopped. There was blood everywhere now. All over Tara's legs and Pleun's front. Soetanto didn't move or say a word but there were tears running down her face and she was shaking. I stood up and looked at Nirmala. She wasn't dead. She was lying on her side, looking at her hands covered in her own blood as if she couldn't work out where it was coming from. Her breathing was shallow like she couldn't get enough air. Pleun was slumping slowly backwards pawing at her throat and trying to breathe like a fish out of water. Tara just kept repeating that she was sorry.

We could hear the men shouting back to Pleun, getting closer. Their footsteps banged on the path and Tara's head jerked up. She stepped over Pleun and ran towards the table, pushing it against the door. I dug in my bag for the shotgun and ran to help her.

"Please help us?" Tara begged Soetanto, but the girl just backed onto a bed and wrapped her knees in her arms, staring at the door and the shotgun and back again. The men kicked against the door and the table jumped but we held it. Tara whispered: she'd let the door open enough for one of them, then trap him while I shot him. I didn't even think twice about how that would have to end for the man. These weren't terrified little girls. I was not getting raped in some shitty mine in Borneo. No fucking way. And that's how it is with me now. No fucks given. Just like Tara.

The first part went better than we could have hoped. I held the shotgun tight and Tara held the table. There was only one shot but there were only two of them and two of us. And we were more desperate than they were.

The door lurched open and one of the miners fell in the across the table before Tara pushed it back. I aimed the shotgun at him and told him to get out. No, I screamed it. He started to lift himself up but he was stuck and he shouted something back at me: I could hear the words for "bitch" and "whore", and I guessed the rest. He kept shouting the same thing and staring at me: not at my face but my body like I was naked and not covered in mud-caked clothes.

I felt his eyes crawl over me like they were his actual hands. I wanted it to stop.

I pulled the trigger. A second later I was lying on the floor with the wind knocked out of me. There were bits of the miner all over the table and the door and Tara and the other miner. The man I'd shot didn't have a face any more. He didn't have much of a head at all. It still seemed to take forever for his body to flop onto the table.

Tara and the last miner and Soetanto all went silent for a minute. I tried to find the breath to scream. My ears were ringing and the shotgun was on the floor between my feet. The last miner saw I'd dropped it and he rushed at the table. It shot back and he flew in. Tara staggered back, crashing against something. That should have been game over for us, but he tripped over the first miner's legs and fell on me. Landed with his face in my tits and knocked the wind out of me again. My head smacked on the floor again. For a minute I couldn't see anything. My ears rang even louder. It was dark and I couldn't breathe and he was pushing me down while he tried to get up.

Then he stopped pushing and my eyes cleared, just a blur first then sharper. Tara stood over us. She was kicking him in the head and she had a lot of anger to work through. Her face looked just like I'd felt when I pulled the trigger, like all the shit she'd been through had found somewhere to go. I couldn't hear but I could see her grunt with every kick. The miner tried to cover his head with one arm every time her foot swung back and kept pushing himself up to get away, but those boots are heavy. Tara wasn't going to stop until her rage was spent.

I stayed on my back so I didn't get kicked and he dropped onto my chest again with both arms around his head. She was so ragey it didn't stop her. I was pinned underneath him but I didn't want to stop her even though she kicked my tit a couple of times. In the end he went limp and I had to shout at Tara to stop kicking.

We should have stopped then. We'd won, right? The miners were all dead, Nirmala was probably dead. We could have stayed there with Soetanto and waited for help. I don't know what we were thinking. We weren't thinking. We were just dead scared and there was blood all over us and none of it was ours.

Tara pushed the dead man off me and pulled me up. She threw the shotgun at me. We grabbed our bags again and ran through the camp. We got in the boat, untied it and sat there drifting back down the river, just holding each other and shaking and crying.

It was too late by the time we saw we'd fucked ourselves. We couldn't start the engine in the dark. We left Soetanto sitting in her bed, crying, surrounded by death. What sort of women are we to leave her behind like that?

So now we're stuck on a boat again and this time there's nowhere left to go. Drifting down the river to Pondok Fucking Bahaya. It's still dark and we've only got a little head torch for writing. Maybe we can sneak in and kill those crazy fuckers before they get us. Is that self defence or is that murder? I don't even care now.

I just want this to end. I hope it's not real. I hope Ibu Intan fed us trippy mushrooms or frogs. If it's not real then it doesn't matter, does it? I fucking hate boats. And trees. I just want to go to sleep and wake up in my bed in England. Next year I'm going to Ibiza.

Diary: Tara Fowler, morning

```
Tara's writing is more legible, but the pages are
splashed with water and smeared with brown
bloodstains.
```

We're almost back to Pondok Bahaya. Maya was so brave to fight off Cristian like that. So brave and so stupid. We truly thought it might be someone coming to help us when we saw another boat coming up the river. Maybe I should have expected the worst, but that's not me. I wouldn't be here if I thought there was no hope.

There was just one person in the boat. At first we didn't recognise him. One naked white guy, covered in blood and dirt and probably his own shit. He looked like a stone age warrior, laughing at us drifting in the river. We had oars but we were just using them to stay in the middle. There was too much current to get back upstream and the banks were blocked. Forest and river plants so thick we couldn't even see how far it was to dry land. Why would we hurry to get to Pondok Bahaya?

Cristian looked astonished when he saw me. Can't remember what we all said but it was something like:

"Tara? Fucking hell bitch, I thought you were dead. Ali will be surprised. Hey Maya. Whose blood is that? Did you have to fight your own battle this time, you abbo-fucking whore?"

"Fuck you Cris. Stay the fuck away from us," said Maya.

"No. You scrubbers have got nowhere to go. I'll give you a rope and you'll come with me." He stood up in the boat, a coil of rope in his hand.

"No fucking way. I saw what you did to Dewi and Rendy. Cutting people and eating them? You're both sick," I said.

"You shouldn't even be alive, you slag. Ali didn't even have her full strength when she got you the first time. She's like a goddess now."

"Is that her or Rimadan?" I asked.

"How the fuck do you know about Rimadan?"

"We've read her fucking diary," said Maya. "She thinks she's possessed. She's a fucking psycho."

He laughed. "You don't know the half of it. It's all true. I saw her in the forest, the night before she beat the shit out of Tara. She met this old shaman guy and came back different. Strong."

"I don't fucking care. You're both fucking mental. Just fuck off and leave us alone." I wasn't my most verbose, but this was weird. I hadn't got to know Cristian, but he didn't seem the type to believe in ghosts. Maya was giving me 'WTF?' looks and trying to quietly work out how to reload the shotgun without Cristian seeing it.

"Straight up, bitches," he protested. "There's this angry thing inside her and all it wants to do is kill people and fuck. Every time she eats human flesh she's just like buzzing with energy. And so horny. So filthy. My dick has never worked so hard." He grabbed his penis, which I'd been trying not to look at, and held it out as if we'd take pity on it.

"So you're just fucking the mentally ill for the edge play sex and a high protein diet, Cris? Put that nasty little worm away." Maya made me laugh.

"Not old and wrinkly enough for you? Shame about your old man," he laughed. "That fucking croc was awesome. Ali made that happen. You'll see."

Cristian's boat was drifting closer to us. I tried to row away, but the river was too narrow and the current was determined to bring us together. There was a click and Maya raised the shotgun out of the boat, aiming it at Cristian's crotch.

"I've had a real man, I don't need a dirty little boy. I said 'fuck off'."

"You're not going to shoot me, little firestarter. I'll teach you what a real man feels like." He lifted his dirty and tumescent penis in her direction, then mine. "Maybe Ali will let me have both of you before we cut you up."

"The fuck you will." There was a click and nothing happened. Cristian laughed.

"Pondok Bahaya's the only place you can go. Now take the rope." He drew his arm back to throw it at us.

"You're not taking us back," I said.

"Your choice bitch. Ali just wants meat and revenge. I'll kill you now and fuck her." He dropped the rope, picked up a machete and pointed at me, then Maya. The boats were so close he'd be able to jump across soon. We weren't even shouting to each other now.

No woman wants to be raped. But Maya has lost her shit fast every time she's felt out of control. I could see it when Cristian grabbed her in the camp that day and when those miners were coming for us. Cristian's words were a trigger. He was ready to jump across but she grabbed an oar and slapped him with it. He teetered, arms windmilling as the narrow boat rocked under him. Maya swung the oar to slap him again but he caught it, grabbed the blade and pulled her over. I reached for Maya but she hung on instead of letting go and tumbled out of the boat.

Cristian went in on top of her, his boat flipping over and filling with water. It was all I could do to stop ours going the same way. Maya tried to get back into our boat but he grabbed her hips and pulled her under until I smacked him on the head with the other oar. She came back up, gasping for air and started swimming for our boat. I grabbed Maya's hand and pulled, trying to get her out without tipping us over. Cristian reached for her legs but his arm froze. He let out this surprised squawk and vanished under the water. No thrashing or blood, just gone. And that was the last I saw of Cristian.

Maya looked around, trying to haul herself across me into the boat, begging me breathlessly to get her out of the water. I grabbed her waist and pulled, hoping the boat wouldn't flip over. Maya was half in when something started biting her legs. I don't think it was a crocodile. I think a croc got Cristian and good fucking riddance to him, but there was something smaller with lots of sharp teeth biting Maya's legs. They weren't hanging on, just biting. I grabbed her, flopped onto my back and she flopped in on top of me, screaming. Something bumped against the boat, again and again as I held her tight. We stopped moving and it must have lost interest.

Slowly I sat us up. Maya's legs are shredded. Dozens of sharp bites. She's bleeding everywhere. I've torn up my clothes for bandages but I can't stop it. She's hardly conscious and the boat's full of blood and water.

She gave me her bracelet. A bunch of cute little charms on a gold chain. Made me put it on so it gets home to her mum and dad. She knows she's going to die. I don't want her to die. I don't want to be left alone out here. I'm scared too.

Shit, I'm sorry Maya. You tried so hard. I thought you were a silly kid, but you're alright. We almost made it back to your exams and cold British weather and KFC. And beer. Almost. I was supposed to look after you all. Me and Rendy were supposed to look after you all.

You and me didn't get on at first but I wouldn't have wanted anyone else by my side these last couple of days. And I think Rangga was a nice guy. She told me all about him last night, how she was going to raise money to get him to England or just come out here to be with him if they got out of this alive. I guess he was a bit of a dirty old man but I think that's just how they expect things to be here, you get a young wife no matter how old you are. He treated her with respect and he tried to save her life. I should be so lucky.

I don't even have the energy to face Alison. Maybe I'll take those last paracetamol for this. Every part of me feels like shit. Even my legs hurt from kicking that fucking miner. I'd let Alison kill me if I thought she'd do it quickly but I saw what she did to the others. She's nasty. She'll want to hurt me. I don't want to have to kill her. I haven't even got anything I could kill her with. It won't even be dark when we get there. When I get there.

Diary: Tara Fowler, afternoon

Adrift again. Well, floating opposite the dock at Pondok Bahaya if I'm being less dramatic, which I don't want to be because…because I've had enough. I've been trying to stay focussed on getting from one day to the next, but it's exhausting and now I'm stuck in this bloody boat. This literally bloody boat. Again!

Cristian wasn't lying about Alison. She's crazy. She might as well be possessed and I don't really believe in anything like that. But what she's done is so far beyond insane that she's either pure evil or she's not in control of herself. I don't want her to be pure evil.
I think she would have tried to kill me when I told her he was dead. Maybe she would have if I didn't have the shotgun. She doesn't know it's broken.

After a lot of screaming — a lot — she agreed to go to the top of the jetty so I could haul Maya's body up the steps. I can't have it in the boat with me but I can see it from here. If she tries any crazy shit, I'll know.

I cried all the way through, but Alison kept her word and let me half-drag, half-carry Maya to the little hut at the bottom of the dock. She looked pleased — smug, even — to see Maya dead, but I think those horrible bites all over Maya's legs might have convinced her that something really did eat Cristian. She looked at them and just went "fuuuuuck".

Afterwards I went back to the end of the dock. She came about halfway down, then sat down. Her body slumped like a rag doll as she stared at me with weird, vacant eyes. I sat down and rested the gun in my lap. I really wanted some shade but at least I still had my hoodie. I asked her if it was true, what Cristian had said about the old man.

Her head kind of snapped up, but her eyes didn't change. When she spoke, it wasn't like the Alison I met when she got here. She slurred a long "yeah". I asked what happened.

"His voice was like the jungle," she said. "It made my head quiet. Not like words, but I had to follow him. I wanted to follow him."

Then what?

"He put Her in me. It took a long time. It felt good. Really, really good." She grinned, stupidly, rubbing her hands through the matted, dirty hair on her head.

Her?

"Rimadan. The Great Hunter. The jungle spirit. From the north. In my head, see? I can't hear me any more." She sighed.

Can't hear me?

"My thoughts. Shouting. Always talking. All I had to do was make Her happy and She kept them quiet."

Make her happy?

"Kill you all. Send you away."

Why?

"Hurting Her land. Not jungle people."

But Rendy and Dewi and the others, they wanted to help the rainforest. We all did.

"Not jungle people. It doesn't want you here. Even when you killed the others. Still not jungle people."

What about Cristian? Why didn't you kill him?

"Ha! Rimadan likes him. When he takes me it makes us both strong. He can't take me any more." That stupid grin flashed across her face, chased away by anger. "Why aren't YOU dead yet?" She swept onto all fours, like a cat poised to pounce.

I grabbed the shotgun and aimed it until she slinked back down, less raggy-doll but relaxed again.

"Why aren't you dead?" The question wasn't aimed at me, this time, and she stared off into the trees. "Have to think about that."

I told her I'd killed people too now. Miners and other people. Just to kill time I told her what had happened in the mining camp. It seemed to amuse her. Or the voice. This Rimadan.

What did I become in that moment when I stabbed the old lady and the girl. Maybe Maya had been scared of me? I hadn't thought about it. There was no time to think and I was so angry they'd betrayed us. I wanted to protect Maya at any cost. Now she was dead and there was no-one left to rescue me. Just Alison and whatever was going on in her head. I wondered if she was adding up the numbers to decide if I should live or die. Or if there really could be something else inside her, judging me. Adding up the numbers for her.

The sun was beating down on my hoodie, and Alison was in the shade. I asked for some water.

"It's a slow death," she said. It was hard to look at her eyes. The sun caught her pupils as she stared at me and I swear I could see them growing and shrinking, from dinner plates to pinpoints and back again. "We want to know why you're not dead. Rimadan doesn't know what you are."

She got up and walked away into the camp. I got into the shade once she was out of sight. I wondered if the hall was still full of disembodied heads. What had she done to Dewi and Rendy? It must be disgusting by now, full of flies and god knows what else. I still don't know what made her torture people and eat them — EAT THEM FFS!!! — before she killed them.

Just when I thought she'd gone for good, she came back down with a water bottle — my water bottle — and a sleeping bag. She put them down and stepped back.

"You can't stay here. I don't know what we'll do to you. What She wants. I don't have any food but I put some sugar in that."

I took the stuff and walked away, then I stopped. "Alison," I said. "I don't really know you but I don't think you wanted to do this. Cristian is dead. Maya's dead. Everyone is fucking dead. Even if you kill me, people will come here and they'll see what you did and they will punish you. This voice — Rimadan — won't stop that. Think about that."

I got back in the boat, rowed across the river and tied myself to a low branch. I need to save the torch tonight and I'm so hungry but I don't know what else to do. I can't go into the camp. She could be waiting for me or she could be off in the forest. At least I've got water. I hope it's clean. It tastes good.

Alison watched me from the dock for a while, then she went back into the camp. She's doing something up there. I can hear her moving things around but I can't see through the trees. That voice in her head could be telling her anything.

I don't want to sit here in the dark but there's nowhere else to go. Even the monkeys don't like me being here. Little shits keeping throwing nut shells at my head. Not nuts I could eat, though, just shells. FML as Maya would have said.

Email: Alan Caudwell to Imogen Nicholson

To: founder@saveorangutans.org.uk
From: alan@caudwell.org.uk
Subject: Pondok Bahaya diaries - August 4-6
Date: 4 September 2018 17:18

I had to hope there was something better than the terrible things they did to Harriet. Some hope for Rendy and Maya and Dewi and Rangga. I'm sorry this is all I can give you.

All I can think of is that if Tara survived being beaten and falling into the river the first time, then maybe she survived whatever Alison was planning. Maybe she tried to find a way home and she's out there somewhere?

I finally got some sleep when they threw me out of the room to clean it. The staff woke me up when the pool emptied for lunch! I'm going to sleep tonight if I can but I'll finish these diaries tomorrow if it kills me! There isn't much left anyway. Alison didn't write any more 'letters' to Manny so it's just a few entries from Tara. At least her writing's easy to read. I've gone cross-eyed deciphering Alison's scrawl.

Alan x

Tuesday, August 7, 2018

Diary: Tara Fowler, late morning

WTF did Alison do last night? I finally found a way to lie down under the sleeping bag with a flat bit of dry boat under me, and the monkeys got bored of dropping stuff. I don't know if there was something in that water or what because I was having crazy dreams — Maya was screaming and I was murdering people with a huge parang and there was blood everywhere and then I was drowning and finally a big klotok came to save us all but there was just me and loony Alison singing "the jungle made me do it" over and over again.

And then I was woken up by the biggest bang I have ever heard. I nearly fell out of my boat. There were flames all over Pondok Bahaya. I tried to get my little boat untied but the rope was caught in the trees. It still felt like a dream but I knew I couldn't swim in the river.

It looked like the whole forest was going to burn up but the sky started to cloud over and it rained. Not a shower. Hard rain, like bullets. I was soaked and the river swelled up, and my boat started to get pulled down the river. All I could think of was going under the water when Alison pushed me in.

I clung onto the tree branches in case my knots didn't hold. I was terrified I'd be dragged into the trees or down the river into that crap where I fell in last time. Even when the rain stopped, the river was a torrent, but I couldn't risk trying to cross the river at night with just one oar. I begged the boat to stay under me. I begged the jungle to save me. I begged God. I begged for my mum and dad to come and save me. And when no-one came I hung on like that tree was the last solid thing in the world. As soon as the sun came up, I paddled like mad to the other side so I could get out of that bloody boat and find out what that mad woman had done.

The good news is the rain has killed most of the fires. The bad news is that Pondok Bahaya is nothing more than three scorched concrete buildings and a big sign on a wooden dock. I don't know how Alison did it, but the main hall and the accommodation block have been blown up and burned down to charred wooden posts. The water tower has burned up and fallen down, or maybe the other way round, and every tree and plant near the camp is scorched. The ground is covered in ashy black mud. Even the concrete buildings have had the doors and windows blown inside. The toilet block was half-demolished when the water tower fell down.

The I-don't-know-if-it's-good-or-bad news is that Alison is still alive. I almost tripped over her! I thought she must have blown herself up, but I found the mad cow flat on her back, half-naked and caked in wet ash and leaves.

She was out cold and that's probably what saved her. Face-to-face, in self-defence, I know I can kick a man to death with my boots, but standing over her defenceless body…I couldn't do it. I know she's dangerous. Maybe she'd do it to me, but I'm not her.

And I'm angry. I'm angry that she killed Rendy and Dewi and Paul and Harriet and sweet old Ibu Intan. I'm angry that she destroyed Pondok Bahaya, a place that exists to help the rainforest, a place that Rendy and the others all loved. I screamed it all at her even though she couldn't hear me.

But there is a cold, logical reason to keep her alive. I'm the only survivor. Who's going to believe me? There must be human remains all over this place. She did that. She has to answer for it. I've got blood on my hands but that was different. I won't take the blame for the things she did here.

I dragged her to Dewi's room and left her on a mattress on the floor. She was always skinny but she's right boney now. I think Alison was planning to use it — there was a bag with Cristian's camera and their phones. And more water and a few packs of sweets she must have scrounged from the rooms. Fucking Skittles! Are they mine or Rendy's? They taste like sweet heaven right now but they make me sad because he's dead. And there's matches! I'll hide those.

I found some rope in the office so I've tied her wrists and I've tied one foot to the bed. It feels cruel the state she's in — all bruises and scratches — but I don't know what else to do. I just hope I can get through to her when she wakes up.

I'll hide the other diaries in one of the office filing cabinets. Maybe I'll read them if I have time. I kind of wish I could read Rendy's, but it's all in Indonesian.

Diary: Alison Pierce, evening

```
Alison's new notebook picks up her story in a
traditional diary format, with a date at the top of
each page. Her trademark nature doodles are still
present, but the intense darkness that took over
her diary-in-letters has been reset to the playful
plants and animals of her arrival. If anything,
there's an added lightness to her hand.
```

OOOOWWWWWW!!!!

Haven't felt this sore since I woke up after my accident. Head hurts. Bruises all over my back and my bum. Cuts and scratches all over my bum and my legs too. I don't know how. Not true. I know how the bruises got there. Don't really know about the cuts but Tara's here in the bedroom. Think she dragged me in here.

Looks like Tara anyway. Confusing. Thought Tara was dead. Won't answer my questions. Doesn't help. She's really angry with me. Really angry. Maybe she thinks I killed her. I think I killed her. Maybe I'm dead. Afterlife looks a lot like a hut in Pondok Bahaya. Being dead hurts like fuck. And I'm naked and covered in dirt. And she's tied me up.

Asked for some clothes and clean water and a towel. Just said I should have thought of that before. Yeah she's really angry.

Took a mo to remember what she was talking about. No clothes left, are there? Or clean water. It's a bit fuzzy, but I remember what I did last night. Don't really understand why. So many questions. What day is it? Where is everyone? Why is Tara so pissed off at me? Sort of remember getting here on a boat. Then I remember last night like a dream. Need my diary. My letters to Manny. Manny! I miss Manny!

Tara gave me this exercise book. Told me to stop asking questions. Write stuff down before it gets dark.

Dark!?

Must have slept all day.

Got to lie on my front. Back hurts a lot. Wish I had some clothes. At least she gave me some biscuits and water. Stole the sweets though.

So last night. Blew up the big hall. Don't really know why. Burned everything in it. Probably a good thing. There were bodies in it. Oh dear. People who were here like Rendy and Dewi and Paul and that little guy. Revo. And the old lady who cooked. All a mess.

Don't know why they're dead. I think I did it. Which is wrong.

I can feel it.

Don't like it.

Don't want to remember.

Dragged the gas bottles from the kitchen to the middle of the hall. Really heavy. Almost dropped one on my foot. Cut my leg. Got all the bedsheets and clothes. Not many left. Weird! Left some in here for myself. Got all the petrol from the generator hut. Poured it over everything.

I was really excited. Felt like someone was encouraging me. Who was that? A voice in my head? There wasn't anyone else here.

I've got no voices now.

Fuck that's nice. So quiet. Just the birds and stuff outside.

I remember Cris. Big hunk. Wanted to fuck him. So thirsty for that body. Think I did. Feel like I've fucked a lot. Where's Cris now? Was dreaming about him when I woke up.

Really really HORNY :P

Not telling Tara about that :o

Don't think she wants to hear me say anything now. Why so angry?

So last night…I lit the fire. Sat in my bedroom door. Watched it burn. Fire spread all over the floor. Up the walls. Into the kitchen tent. And the food store. Up the water tower. The roof fell in. Waited for the gas bottles to get really hot and blow it all up. Fire was going really well.

Now I remember!

I wanted to get closer. Guess I got too close. Gas bottles exploded. Knocked me out.

Getting too dark to write now.

I'm tired. Everything really hurts.

But no voices. Haven't felt this peaceful inside my head for years and years. Not since my accident.

One more biscuit and sleep sleep sleep.

Diary: Tara Fowler, evening

I read Alison's diary again. It was too much to take in the first time. Just knowing she'd gone mad was enough to get me though when I found Harriet and saw them torturing Dewi and Rendy. What happened to them? Their bodies must be in the wreckage, somewhere. Or everywhere after that explosion.

How much did they suffer? Only Alison knows now. Did they eat them, like Harriet? I feel sick thinking about it. Dewi was so pleasant, so helpful. She loved this place. And Rendy, this was his home, more than anywhere else. Stupid lug telling me he fancied me. What was he thinking?!

So is Alison schizo or bipolar or split personality or what? Cristian seemed to think she was possessed but that's just bollocks. I know she had something wrong with her head before she got here but she was the one who attacked me in my hammock and then she tried to kill me in the boat.

Even after what Cristian said I thought she'd just had a freak out but she wanted me to drown. She said there was something IN HER HEAD that made her do it but how does that make it better? What if it's still there? I mean, what if she thinks it's still there?

How do I know she's not going to try to kill me again when she gets her strength back?

At least she won't be going anywhere today. It's a miracle she didn't break anything in the explosion but she's moaning that everything hurts and her back is cut and scratched. She deserves so much worse. And she's acting like she didn't do anything.

Where am I Tara?
Why am I tied up Tara?
Why does everything hurt Tara?
Where is everyone Tara?
I'm hungry Tara!

I didn't believe she knew nothing so I got one of the exercise books from the office and threw it at her and told her to write down what she did last night if she could remember anything. I wanted to scream at her. For a minute I wanted to kill her. But if I lose my shit there's no-one left to tell people what happened. I have to believe someone will come for us soon and I need to keep her alive to answer for this. So I ran down to the dock and screamed and cried on my own.

I could sleep in the office or the boat or maybe in the birdwatching tower but I don't want to let her out of my sight. She can barely reach for a drink of water now and I've got the only light. If anything comes in the night it will eat her first!

Wednesday, August 8, 2018

Diary: Tara Fowler, morning

Last night I thought I was having a dream about someone having sex in the room. I woke up and Alison was moaning and talking. I heard Cristian's name and it dawned on me that she was dreaming about sex. I've never heard anyone else's sex talk and those were details I do not want to know. How long am I going to have to put up with this?

It was getting light so I went outside. I scared something in the ruins of the hall, probably a big lizard or something. To think this all started with Alison seeing an animal one morning and freaking out. Except she didn't. She made it all up! But an old man in the forest? A ghost in her head? How is that any better?

I wish I could sleep outside again. I loved sleeping in my hammock! But every time I think of the hammock I think about waking up with someone kicking me. Only now I know it was Alison and I've got to share a room with her because it's just us.

I slept in the jungle all those nights after I almost drowned — after Alison almost drowned me! Blowing up the hall has probably scattered bits of burned bodies all over the camp. I suppose that's better than all those bodies rotting in the open like Harriet. We should bury her. I'll have to do it, won't I? The thought of finding her — it still makes me feel sick. Maybe I should make Alison do it. If I only knew how.

I can't help thinking about the two of them killing Paul and then Harriet and Dewi and Rendy. And not just killing them. I'm glad she stopped writing her diary after Paul.

One bright spot this morning — a female orangutan and her infant came through the trees by the river. I was sitting on the dock, probably I fell asleep for a bit, and something woke me. The young one was making a noise because the mummy wouldn't let it come down to get a closer look at me, and I just looked back up into two pairs of beautiful deep dark eyes. It's the happiest I've been in weeks. I felt so sad and lonely when the mother started moving off. I think I cried for about an hour and I must have drifted off. I just know it was a lot brighter when I heard Alison calling.

I need to start surviving or this place will kill me without her help. I've got shelter. Now I need fire. There's still loads of wood for a fire. Water. Food. This won't last forever. Someone will come for us.

Alison's been shouting for a bit now. I'd better see how she is.

Diary: Alison Pierce, afternoon

Oh fuck. Fuck fuck fuck what did I do?

Now I know why Tara's so angry. She read what I wrote last night. Threw it back at me. Gave me my own diary to read. Alison's Exotic Adventures. I know it's mine. Manny gave it to me. Lovely Manny.

When did I write all this?

I almost killed her in the hammock. It was pure hate, from nowhere. Like pure white fire inside me. Then I pushed her in the river. And then Paul.

Dreamed of Cris last night. Not a dream though. Read about it now. Memories. His lips on mine. Skin against my skin. Hands around my arms. Inside me. Holy fuck coming so hard. Think I moaned in my sleep. Not sure now I'm awake.

What do I know?

Memories I can trust.

Living in London with sweet Manny. The voices all the time. Coming here on the boat. Orangutans at Camp Pail. The big male so close to me.

Memories I can't trust.

We didn't just kill them. Tortured them. We ate people. Worse. Worse than that. Why? That's not me. I know my own hunger. Not ashamed of that. But those things?

Now it's all I can think of. They screamed and I wanted it.

Killing Paul or Harriet or Dewi or Rendy. I remember the feeling. Walking in the forest. The old man. Fucking Cris. Paul's blood on my skin. The taste of him. The taste of Harriet.

Better than a taste. Strength. Power. So fucking horny. I was a goddess. I would do anything to stay like that.

Something else, too. Someone else with me.

Rimadan.

The she-leopard.

Living in me. Sat on my shoulders. Claws in my skin. Her power. Made my voices go away. It was her power. Made me feel strong. So much pleasure. Made me ache for more. Made me hungry. Hungry like I would starve if I didn't obey Her. She hated everyone. Where did She go? What if She comes back? Don't want that. Too much. No voices now. No mad thoughts. Don't need Her. Don't want Her.

Everything still hurts like fuck. Naked under this sheet. Need to pee. Need to get outside. Need to talk to Tara. Most of all.

Rimadan's still in me. Scratching at my head. She's trapped.

Talk to Tara before She finds a way out.

Need to explain this. Why hasn't Tara killed me? Tried to kill her. Twice. She came back. Saved Maya from me. Maya died. Cris died, she says. Everyone died. Not Tara.

Maybe she can't be killed.

Maybe she's an angel?!!

Maybe she can save me?

Diary: Tara Fowler, evening

The water's boiling slowly. I found one of Ibu Intan's big pans, blown into the trees. It's all dents but no holes. Alison's sleeping again so I may as well catch up in case I have to leave this diary behind.

Alison begged me to let her out. She looked so pathetic, so helpless. I untied her legs and she crawled. Actually crawled like a child, out of the room. She crawled behind the hut, I guess she pee'd, and then she crawled back to me. I thought I looked bad in the mirror at the mining camp, but she is far worse. Cuts and scratches all over her back, black ash mess and bruises all over the front of her. She looks like shit, and sometimes I wonder why I'm keeping her alive, let alone washing her and finding her clothes. I've made my choice and I'm sticking to it.

Now she's gone and made it complicated by asking for my help. She says she knows what she did and she knows she will never be able to apologise for it all, but there was something controlling her and she's scared that it will come back. I don't know if I should believe her or not. She sounds like she believes it. But after Jason I know I'm a sucker sometimes.

And I believe what she told me about the whole world just being too loud — even her own thoughts — after she was in an accident a few years ago. I don't know if I believe her story that sex was the only thing that made it stop so she's been kind of living a double life ever since with all these one night stands and wild parties. But maybe I'm just jealous. I work hard and all I had to show for it was a lying bastard fiancé who almost gambled it all away and sends me death threats. She sleeps around and goes swinging with her boyfriend and he sounds like he's cracked about her.

The bit about the insomnia when she got here, I know that happened. She was scared she'd made a mistake coming here and the noise in her head was worse than ever. I saw all that in her face even if she didn't tell us.

Then she says something happened in the forest one night and there was just one voice. A woman. She calls her Rimadan. She's a jungle spirit or something. When Alison did the things it wanted she felt more than just peaceful — blissful and thirsty for more. It was like a drug, she said. Like cocaine and ecstasy all in one. What do I know about that, good little business woman? Nothing harder than gin or champagne for me. So she killed people and tortured them and ate them and fucked Cristian like there was no tomorrow and every time she did it she felt like a goddess and she didn't want it to stop. But she says Rimadan said that if she stopped she'd lose it all and go back to what it was like before.

I'd like to believe her. Possessed by a jungle spirit? I think she believes it. Maybe Revo and Bimo would have believed her. Definitely Ibu Intan. But she could just be fucking insane.

She knows she's guilty and she'll be punished and she's scared of that, but she says Rimadan is coming back and she's more scared that she'll make her hurt me. She wants to get Rimadan out of her head and to do that, we have to find Rimadan's people. Somewhere in the north. She doesn't know how she knows that, but she says she's sure.

I get that she's scared they won't help her if we're rescued. They'll hurt her and fill her full of drugs and Rimadan or whatever it is will still be inside her. She's terrified. Snot and tears terrified. Even so it sounds like bollocks. I want to go home. She can't even walk. How are we going to find some tribe of jungle people and ask them for help? Why am I even thinking about this? She's mentally ill. She killed people. She almost killed me.

OK, imagine this was just another business decision:

a) Wait for help. Hope Alison doesn't kill me. Probably starve to death anyway.
b) Kill Alison, wait for help and hope they don't think I killed everyone. Probably starve.
c) Help Alison. Maybe Alison kills me. Maybe we starve in the jungle.

All the options are shit. I don't want to starve to death. I don't want Alison to kill me. I don't want to die at all. I don't want to kill Alison. I don't want to be blamed for everything. I killed people and there's a witness. Why would they believe me?

I suppose that means option C is the least shit. Another bloody walk in the jungle. At least I've still got my boots.

Thursday, August 9, 2018

Diary: Tara Fowler, morning

I didn't sleep much. Again. Alison didn't wake me up this time — it was dreams about killing people and watching Maya die. When I went to sleep Alison was talking to herself and when I woke up it had turned into a furious one-sided argument. I couldn't tell what she was saying but she kept trying to knock something off her shoulders. It got pretty agitated and then…more sex dreams. The moaning is one thing, but suddenly I can hear every word!! I can't imagine Cristian was that obedient in real life, but he does what he's told when she's dreaming. I wish I had orgasms like that — shaking and flushed pink. No wonder she went for it with every man. And afterwards she slept so quietly I could only just hear her breathing. Even asleep she's having a better life than me.

This morning she's perky as hell and a lot more mobile. The bruises and scratches look a lot better and she's strolling around with the sheet wrapped around her like a dress. I'd say she looks even more skinny, though.

She ran off into the jungle while I was boiling water and came back with a handful of fruit. She says they're good to eat. I don't have any choice. Those tasteless Belvita biscuits Maya left behind won't keep us alive.

And then she drops the bomb. Rimadan is back in her head. They 'spoke' last night while we were sleeping. So that's what I heard. What came afterwards was kind of a payment — I'm not sure who was paying who. Anyway, they've made a deal: Alison says Rimadan is going to take us to a shaman who can find it someone new to live in, in return for keeping her alive. It's kind of implied that it won't tell Alison to hurt me if we go, and I don't like the idea of sprightly Alison around me if we stay here and it gets angry.

I'm not saying I buy the whole 'possessed' thing, but if she believes it then I've got to go along with it. Rimadan seems like a partner now, and that's a better kind of crazy than something making her kill people.

I've told her we need a day to boil and bottle as much water as we can carry. She's going to find fruit and nuts we can eat to build up our strength. Maybe she'll even find something I could cook. I would kill for a potato right now!

※ ※ ※

I'm not excited about Alison walking around with a parang or a hoe, but she came back with something big and brown, peeled and chopped it and told me to boil it. It was really starchy and dry but I haven't felt this full since we ate that meal at the mining camp.

Poor Maya. Why am I stuck with this nutter instead of you? Did we go through all of that shit to be walking off into the jungle again?

Diary: Alison Pierce, midday

Rimadan came back.

Dreamed I was in the forest. Leopard walked up to me. Knew it was Her. I wasn't scared. Nervous. Purred around my legs. Jumped on my shoulders. Not heavy. Soft and silky. Her words make me tingle inside when she's happy. Numb and cold when she's angry. Not English but I understand.

Wants me to leave Pondok Bahaya. Go into the jungle. Told me to kill Tara. Run away. Wants to find Her people. They have a shaman. Come out of my head into someone else. Not supposed to be in me. Old man sick and lost. Supposed to give Her to someone new. Used me when he died. Old man was Her… Don't know the word. Like a horse but… don't think they have horses here. A hunter too. Someone strong. Stealthy. Skilled. Someone Rimadan can ride. Don't know how to be what She wants. Supposed to make each other happy.

I'm not right. Think too much. Feel too much. Too many questions. Didn't question Her when She stopped my voices. Different now.

I don't want to kill Tara. Tara can't be killed.

Rimadan was angry when I said that. Said I'd be dead without Her.

I said I'd be mad and unhappy without Her, but nobody would be dead. We can find Her a new Hunter. Tara's coming with us. Said I'll stay here if she tries to make me hurt Tara. I think She believed me. Was so scared but it worked. She's doing what I want. I feel powerful.

I know something she doesn't. She doesn't care about my diary being gone. Doesn't understand what I do when I'm writing. All just shapes to her. Scratches on paper.

Don't trust Her. I like sex. Needed the sex. Wanted my voices to stop. Didn't want to like killing people. She made me like that. Made me want to do it. Made it feel like sex. Better than sex. And my voices have gone. Think She knows that. Don't need Her like I did before. Must be a good Hunter.

Friday, August 10, 2018

A letter to our rescuers

```
This note was found on the desk, inside the office
building at Pondok Bahaya. Unfortunately, the
rangers then tucked it into the back of Tara's
diary for transport. Having photographed every page
in a hurry to pass the diaries to the authorities,
I didn't realise its importance until I reached the
end of my transcription.
```

Hi,

If you've found this then you've made it to Pondok Bahaya. You're too late. Everyone here is dead except for Alison Pierce and myself. I can't explain how it all happened, but the diaries in the filing cabinet will tell you our story.

I can't say where we're going or when we'll come back. I can't say because I'm not 100% sure. I don't even know if we'll come back. I hope I'm doing the right thing. Tell my mum and dad I love them.

Don't blame Rendy or Dewi or the OST. They did the best they could.

Tara Fowler, volunteer coordinator
Pondok Bahaya, Kalimantan, Borneo. 10th August 2018

Email: Imogen Nicholson to Alan Caudwell

To: alan@caudwell.org.uk
From: founder@saveorangutans.org.uk
Subject: Re: Pondok Bahaya diaries - is this the end?
Date: 5 September 2018 15:50

Poor Tara. Did she really think she'd be held responsible for everything that she did? That night at the mining camp must have been terrifying, coming after everything else she'd been through. If she could forgive Alison for all that she did, then surely we could forgive her?

I only wish that we had seen her letter to the rescuers when we started. I suppose it was picked up with all the other diaries when they came back. It's almost a month now since they left Pondok Bahaya. They could be anywhere in the rainforest. It only gets more wild as you go further North. The rangers told me there is primary rainforest up there that only the indigenous Dayak have been in. There are still rumours of groups that have little or no contact with modern-day Indonesians, living nomadically.

I want to look for her but it's up to the Indonesian authorities now. I'll tell them what I know, although I'm sure they won't be happy that we have copies of everything.

I cannot thank you enough, Alan. I had no idea what I would be asking you to look at when I asked for your help. You have been a true friend to me, and I haven't even been able to say hello in person. Can you come over to the offices tomorrow? I feel that you should be there when I break the news to my team. They deserve to know what happened to their friends and family.

Forget the restaurant. I'll make dinner afterwards. It's the least I can do.

Jenny xx

Email: Alan Caudwell to Imogen Nicholson

To: founder@saveorangutans.org.uk
From: alan@caudwell.org.uk
Subject: Re: Re: Pondok Rahaya diaries - is this the end?
Date: 5 September 2018 18:44

I'll be happy to back you up tomorrow and answer any questions that I can.

I thought I'd sleep all day but I've started thinking of how I'd compile all of the diaries into a story that makes sense. It's the journalist's curse! There's a lot of times where everyone writes about the same events, so I'll try to use the most helpful account unless they disagree.

I need a couple of days to recharge, but I want to get started while it's all fresh. I have a feeling you'll need it sooner than later.

See you tomorrow. It's been too long.

Alan x

Surrender

Monday, September 10, 2018

Email: Imogen Nicholson to Alan Caudwell

To: alan@caudwell.org.uk
From: founder@saveorangutans.org.uk
Subject: The search is off
Date: September 10 2018 10:32

Hope you had a good flight, hon. Wish you could have stayed for longer.

Pak Rafi called yesterday. The Indonesian police are winding up their search for Tara and Alison. They will be declared missing, presumed dead.

To be honest, I'm surprised they kept looking for this long. The whole thing will be blamed on a dispute with the miners that got out of hand. The local politicians are jumping on it to score political points over those illegal mines, the foreign workers and the poor women who end up with them. Maybe something good will come out of it, one day. I have to believe that it will.

The diaries and the laptops and everything else are a complication, so PR thinks we might get them back. I don't know what we'll do with them, but at least they'll be in a safe place. The lawyers and trustees have your digest of the diaries. I'll let them decide what we should tell the families. I honestly can't decide whether I'd want to know that my loved ones suffered as much as Harriet or Dewi or Rendy.

I'm still mulling those offers from the other orangutan charities. It would be the ultimate disaster if the orangutans and their rainforest suffers because of this. My team in Kalimantan need to know that their work will continue and they will still be paid. Even with our insurance, there will be nothing left of the OST when everyone has got what they deserve. We have six other field stations and the reserve to keep going, but we've worked alongside those other charities for years now. The reserve will be in good hands.

It's just, it's hard to admit that this part of my life is over. By the time the police, the coroners, the public inquiry and the damned media have finished with me, I'll be too toxic for any charity over here. Maybe I should get back into field work, somewhere remote. Just me and the apes.

I feel calmer already, thinking about it. You'd come and say hello, wouldn't you?

Jenny xx

Acknowledgements

THIS BOOK would not exist without the Orangutan Foundation, with whom I spent a wonderful and entirely non-murderous three weeks in the Borneo rainforest with a group of lovely permanent staff and my fellow volunteers. As volunteers, our task was to rebuild the hall at Pondok Ambung, the visitor centre and research station on which Pondok Bahaya is based. I hope that our inexpert DIY skills provided at least as much help as they did hindrance. Unlike my fictional volunteers, we were fortunate to see wild orangutans on several occasions, but the real gift was a glimpse into the invaluable work that the Orangutan Foundation performs to protect the dwindling Borneo rainforest and all of its inhabitants. Please visit www.orangutan.org.uk and support them.

I must thank Nanowrimo for the challenge of writing a 50,000-word first draft in one month, which provided the spring from which Blood River flowed.

Since then, many eyes have helped me to understand my story: Martin Ouvry and my fellow writers on his 2018 Introduction To The Novel short course at City University, London; Jonathan Gibbs, Russell Schechter and my fellow writers on the MA in Creative Writing: The First Novel at St Mary's University, Twickenham; and Laura, Rob, Alan and Jamie, who told me everything that was wrong with my final drafts.

Sharon's creativity is a daily inspiration. And my apologies go to Bongo and Sandy, who fell at the final edit.

About the author

ALEXANDER LANE has almost died on several continents. When he's not wondering whether scuba diving is truly as safe as it is incredible, he's planning his next trip to somewhere that's hopefully more fun than fatal, and dreaming of the many ways that space travel could be both wonderful and dangerous. He always buys good travel insurance, and so should you.

He graduated with a distinction from the creative writing MA at St Mary's University, Twickenham, in 2020, and currently lives in Ireland, where there are no snakes or large predators.

Visit his website at www.alexanderlane.co.uk.